Warning

This Is A Test.

This Is Only A Test.

Gloria Favors

Copyright © 1998
By: Gloria Favors / Vision Ministries

All rights reserved under international copyright law. Contents of this publication may not be reproduced, stored in an electronic system, or transmitted in any form or by any means, electronic, mechanical, photocopying, recording or otherwise without the prior written permission of the author.

All Scripture quotations are from the King James Version of the Holy Bible.

First printing, 1998
ISBN: 1-57502-727-5

Printed in the USA by

3212 East Highway 30 • Kearney, NE 68847 • 1-800-650-7888

Acknowledgments

To God be the Glory.

To my husband, Jimmy, for encouragement, support and for believing in me, thank you.

To my Pastor's wife, and dear friend, Cora Lee Anderson. What would I do without you?

Special thanks to Esther Harmon R. N., for your patience, prayers, and medical advise.

To Dottie Jones, my sister, and friend, thank you for all your encouragement.

Aliesha Burks, for your editing skills, and prayers of support, thank you.

Roy Sr. and Cindy Dunn, thank you for being you. You'll never know how much I appreciate you both.

Linda Pixler, thank you for your help in editing and your prayers.

Warning

This Is A Test.

This Is Only A Test.

Preface

There is no life without trials, there is no victory without struggle, there is no joy without sadness, and there is no tomorrow without today. It is for the trials, struggles, sadness, and today that I am grateful.

This story will reveal that the Arrington's bout with the enemy, is not unlike your own. We've all been at what we felt was the end of our rope, and will most likely visit there again.

My hopes are that each page of this book will stir up the faith that is within each of you, to believe that you not only can, but that you will rediscover your weapon of prayer, and by using it realized the awesome impact it can have in your person life. The name of Jesus can not be defeated.

Gloria Favors

James 1:2-6

2   My brethren, count it all joy when ye fall into divers temptations;

3   Knowing this, that the trying of your faith worketh patience.

4   But let patience have her perfect work, that ye may be perfect and entire, wanting nothing.

5   If any of you lack wisdom, let him ask of God, that giveth to all men liberally, and upbraideth not; and it shall be given him.

6   But let him ask in faith, nothing wavering. For he that wavereth is like a wave of the sea driven with the wind and tossed.
(KJV)

Warning. This Is A Test. This Is Only A Test.

The Warning

1

On a foggy, East Texas, December evening, as the sun begins to set, things in the Arrington family seem to be going about the same as usual. Which is not to say all is well, you understand, but the Arringtons are not the type of people to let hard times ruin their day. They have been in the heat of the battle, against the dark side before, and know what it is like to tighten their belts and make things work. So tighten is what they are going to do.

For some very painfully obvious reason, the cliché that comes to mind more and more often lately is, "Due to a shortage, it seems the light at the end of the tunnel has been turned off."

They have been expecting the forces of hell to raise up its ugly head against their home. Already, the Church, those in leadership, and its members have been under a barrage of attacks. Sickness has bombarded families. Financially strapped has most assuredly taken on a whole new meaning since this war began. Emotions, and patience have been tested beyond what was considered the breaking point, and what was once believed to be solid marriages, have been reduced to battle fields. Confusion, bitterness, strife, envying, and every evil work has been working around the clock, hammering away at the foundation of this rural community, and the Church of the Living God. For most of the year the war has been fought collectively, but now the onslaught from the dark side is trying to break down the strongholds of the christian, by attacking each individual family. The enemy knows there is strength in numbers.

Now the enemy's focus seems to be on the Arringtons. Secure in the God they serve, they feel victory is on its way, and they certainly have no intention of giving up now. Marching to victory in the heat of the battle is exactly where they want to be. The only way to deal with the enemy of your soul is to face him head on and don't ever give up.

There is no reward in quitting, but there is honor in finishing this race.

Mitch Arrington is a mechanic, working for the Shepherd County Road Commission in Precinct 4. Tinkering with motors, machinery of any size, or anything with moving parts, has been a hobby of Mitch's since he was a very small boy. He loves to take things apart, examine their working parts, and

Warning. This Is A Test. This Is Only A Test.

put them back together again. If the toaster was missing, his mom always knew right where she could find it. It wasn't necessary for things to be broken for Mitch to want to fix them. He had an inquiring mind that caused him to want to find out what makes things work, and a gift for making everything work better. His parents were grateful they only had one boy; the other four children were girls.

He still loves the sound of the engines when they are tuned just right, the challenge of each new project, the smell of the machinery, and the feel of accomplishment when he is able to make things work. He knows this is a God given talent and takes great pride in his work.

Victoria Arrington has her work cut out for her, with two small, adorable children at home. Chase is a five year old carbon copy of his father and a typical boy. He has his Father's opaque blue eyes, jet black hair, and that distinctive way of walking. He has also inherited the desire for fixing things, or in his case, it's breaking things. For him to actually fix something may take a few more years.

Nicole is barely three and an angel if there ever was one. She has long blonde hair that resembles spun gold, her Mother's award winning smile, and petite facial features. The four make up a happy family.

The Arringtons aren't wealthy people; maybe, you can say, they are middle class. They live within their means and enjoy life as though they had it all. For them, family, means sticking together no matter what comes or how tough the road gets; they are in this Christian Army for keeps. They are trusting in God and holding to their belief that clean living always pays off.

Over the horizon, in the spiritual realm, the power of light and the forces of darkness are about to have an unfriendly discussion, which is most likely the reason for the heavy fog and the muggy feeling in the air. The Arrington's guardian angels, Gunther, a choleric, valiant, warrior, and Kreig, the melancholy, German, have been expecting a visit from the demonic forces. While standing watch they are distracted by a pungent, sulfuric stench that seems to be overtaking the atmosphere. As they turn to investigate, their answer is too close for comfort. It is one of the 'deranged - vagrants - from - the - dark - side.

As the obnoxious beast opens his hissing lips, slime, and a foul odor, gushes forth. "The imps that I have sent to keep watch, and bring me word of a likely target here in this backward town, have brought favorable reports to me. The time is right, and I now know just how I can put a stop to this praying, worshipping, grievous band of christians." His words are thrown at the heavenly warriors arrogantly, and with a twist of glee in his surly voice, he continues to boast. "I've come with orders to make things rougher for the Arringtons."

With confidence, and assurance, Gunther's baritone voice rumbles across the heavens as he puts

Warning. This Is A Test. This Is Only A Test.

the impish, slime ball in his place. "I'm well aware of your orders, Drate. Long before you were ever given permission to test these mortals, your traitorous master had to get permission from The Creator. Now be gone with you, and don't forget, I'm watching your every move." Gunther has been in many battles and altercations with this one. He knows to watch his front, and back side at all times.

Drate sneers and snidely remarks, "I have my orders, and as far as I'm concerned, you can watch me all you want, because that's all you will be able to do!" His voice dripped with sarcasm.

Even the demons of hell know God has **all** power over all the Heavens and the earth. His will is ultimate and supreme.

"Remember the last time you tried to change the orders and do more than your job? You still carry the scar on your scowling face I see!" Gunther pauses, giving the demon time to recall their last meeting.

Drate snarls, and quickly turns his head away from the inquisitive eyes of the two warriors. This scar has been a constant reminder and tremendous humiliation for this once, self-proclaimed demon.

"I let you off **easy** that time, but that was then and this is now. I don't need much more than a hint of a reason to take you out. **I hope I'm making myself clear.**" Gunther's baritone voice is carried across the sky for the world to hear. No one in their right mind would dare tempt Gunther's wrath. Or will they?

As Drate slithers off toward the Arrington's home, rubbing his crusty hand over the scar he despises so much, the night air is left with a bone chilling dampness. Insults and personal attacks don't bother him for too long. He's so stuck on himself he can't see his faults or shortcomings, and if he does, he immediately convinces himself otherwise. "Yea, yea, I know, you're always **gonna** do something!" He taunts, as he's leaving. He always thinks he has to have the last word.

Just as he said, Gunther, accompanied by his trusted friend Kreig, is following the unmistakable trail of the impish little demon. The angelic hosts are well aware of the damage that can be caused by letting one of these demolition types loose on an unsuspecting world. They destroy everything in their path and call it having fun.

There is going to be BIG trouble.

The Hosts from Heaven are set on go. All they require now is the prayers of the believers empowering their efforts. Unfortunately, trouble always finds its way into the lives of those who pray. The forces of hell can't compete against prayer once it's been prayed, but they've had some success through the years at discouraging the mortals, thus keeping them from praying. If the prayer warrior stops praying, the enemy has, in effect, controlled the power of prayer, and has power over the believer. Prayer is the power behind faith.

Warning. This Is A Test. This Is Only A Test.

Gunther has a healthy dislike for Lucifer's army, and he proudly displays it every chance he gets. "When will these insignificance ever learn?" Gunther mumbles to himself. "They are here only because the Master allows them to fulfill their duties." Gunther doesn't give time for anyone to respond, he knows the answer. "Like their evil minded, controlling dictator they so eagerly serve, they can't seem to understand that it's only a matter of time before all is fulfilled and the Holy One says, '**enough**.' Until then, however, we have our job to do, and thanks to the dedication of the Arringtons, our job is made easier."

The Arringtons will sleep little tonight. Drate is going to see to that. One of his favorite pastimes is picking on, as he so boastfully puts it, those tiny little humans, messing with their minds, and causing problems. He doesn't give them time to settle into a deep sleep before he starts the wheels turning in Mitch's mind. Injecting darts of sedating drugs into Mitch's mind helps Drate to work undetected. Once the victim begins to doubt himself, or the things he believes to be facts, the enemy has an avenue to drive his truck full of evil right onto, and park. Drate's not much on face to face, man to man, combat. He likes to hit and run. With his bag of tricks spread out before him, facts from their past, lies about their future, and knowledge of their weaknesses, Drate begins the night of torment. Much like a pesky mosquito loose in the house at night, buzzing, biting, and pestering them in their sleep, Drate will start with the small stuff and work his way up to the bigger things.

"Let the dreams begin!" Drate cackles, as his grip on Mitch's mind tightens.

Thoughts of bills, future financial insecurity, his family's present needs, and the usual burdensome responsibilities of the head of the house, are being magnified in his eyes, courtesy of Drate. Tossing, turning, and thrashing about, he's so tired he can't stand himself, but he can't fall asleep either. Lying in bed only seems to make things worse. Maybe a stroll through the house, a glass of water, and a peek in at the children will clear his head. Knowing he needs to try to get some sleep, he returns to bed. He only gets as far as the edge of the bed, when his attention is drawn to the window. He sees his reflection and what he sees looking back at him is startling. He recognizes himself, but it looks like he's eighty years old, and in very poor health. The reflection has deep set, dark, baggy, eyes, worry lines on his face, and from his countenance, he carries the weight of the world on his shoulders. The look of death hangs like a shroud on this man before him. His mind is being saturated with more self-doubt and discouragement.

Drate's creative juices are really flowing tonight.

"Let me just have one minute with him, Master!" Gunther wants to do what he's been sent to do - guard and protect this battered subject.

"In time," is the response he receives.

Warning. This Is A Test. This Is Only A Test.

Drate's claws dig deeper into the central nervous system. With an accusing tone, to his already offensive sounding voice, he begins to degrade and belittle Mitch. "What a loser you've turned out to be! You could've had so much, been '**somebody**', but no, you wanted to do the Christian thing!" With his little gold hammer, he's pounding, chipping away at Mitch's confidence and self-worth. "Well, Mr. Mechanic, I hope you're proud of yourself. Just look at you!" Drate isn't going to give much space for clear thinking. "Your poor family is having to do without simply because of you. All that talk about being a good provider, where's that gotten you?" Tormenting and harassing - these are his specialties.

Kreig nudges Victoria awake from her sound sleep. He knows Mitch needs someone to help him focus on the cause of this restless night he's having.

Gunther's hands are tied, for now.

She wakes up aware that something is wrong, but what? Her first thought is for the children. She brushes her hair back, props herself up on her elbow, and asks, "Mitch, what's the matter? Can't you sleep?" Victoria leans across the bed where her husband is sitting up, gazing out the window. "It's midnight and you haven't slept any?"

She doesn't get a reply from Mitch, but she does hear the cackling of Drate. She is now sitting straight up, and paying close attention to what is forcing it's way into their lives.

Mitch, unaware of the darts that have been so carefully driven into his brain, finds it hard to separate fact from fiction. He's exhausted, but still unable to turn off the vivid thoughts that flood his mind. He breathes a sigh, "Oh, Jesus," holding his hurting head in his hands.

Gunther hears the call and responds; he's by Mitch's side, making sure the boundaries that are set haven't been breached. "Drate, you're treading on thin ice here." His voice resembles a thunderous blast, as he stands staring down the crooked nose of his enemy. "You have been granted one attempt at destroying Mitch Arrington, and unless you are planning on scaring the man to death, or boring him with your parlor tricks, then I suggest you **back-off**." He has no tolerance with the demons from Lucifer's camp.

Kreig makes his services available to his fellow warrior and is ready to pitch in if need be.

Released from the vice like grip of Drate's infectious claws, Mitch continues holding his aching head in his hands, rubbing his forehead. "I'm not sure what the problem is, but it'll be okay. Go back to sleep, Darling." He slowly inhales a lung full of fresh air, exhales making a puffing sound, climbs back into the bed and tries to relax.

Job 7:13-15

13 When I say, My bed shall comfort me, my couch shall ease my complaint;

14 Then thou scarest me with dreams, and terrifiest me through visions:

15 So that my soul chooseth strangling, and death rather than my life.

(KJV)

Warning. This Is A Test. This Is Only A Test.

Dreams

2

At the mention of that **Mighty Name, Jesus**, demons must flee. With some persuasive prodding from Gunther, Drate decides to find something else to do for the next few hours. His level of bravery is somewhere close to zero, and running is always his answer to confrontations that have the potential of causing him any personal discomfort. Fortunately for him, his level of common sense is not quite as low.

Mitch will now be able to get some badly needed sleep. Drate has better things to do tonight. His plans are to take care of this mortal tomorrow.

Making his exit, he hears a noise off to the North, and is just nosy enough to find out what it is. Being nosy is also one of his favorite pastimes.

Trying his best to put space in between himself and Gunther, he comes to a thick wooded area. The smell of smoke, the glow of a campfire against the dark night sky, the sounds of laughter and horse play, catch his attention. Drawing closer, finding a break in the tree line, he can see a group of young men. The objectives of his search. "Looks like they are camping out. Time for a little fun!" He thought, sneaking in quietly, not wanting to be noticed. He positions himself out of sight while he decides which of his many tricks will be best to play on these unsuspecting young men.

Too bad for him, he is noticed and considered an unwelcome guest by two very large, and determined warriors, Kovec, and Hans, from the throne of Glory. Things just aren't working out for poor Drate tonight. But then, for him, this is how things always work out.

Still thinking he's entered the camp unnoticed, Drate is ready to pull off his first stunt, when he's taken by surprise. Seemingly from out of nowhere, a huge blinding white light sends him to his knees. He crosses his arms in front of his face and tries to shield himself. He has a very large, natural, yellow streak running down his back. His courageous, or tough guy act, is only evident when he has the advantage, and is facing a much smaller, and much weaker opponent.

Hans speaks to the shivering creature crouched on the ground. "Look what we have here, Kovec. It's one of the **b-a-d guys,** and he must have lost his way!" Hans jokingly smiles and pretends to be afraid. "Oh, no, don't let him get me! I'm afraid of the big bad demon." Hans leans back and has a big belly laugh. His tone changes, and with authority he demands, "Show yourself before I have the pleasure of disintegrating you where you crouch." His posture is the personification of confidence and courage.

Warning. This Is A Test. This Is Only A Test.

This is something exciting and new for Kovec; he's only been assigned to guarding mortals a short while. Standing back and taking it all in, he's learning something about handling the demons up close and personal. Although Drate is not a good example for anyone to judge the demonic forces by, he's here and they will make quick work of him. On a scale from one to ten, he is a one half, when it comes to having any leverage in the demonic realm.

Lucifer has no one to depend on; he's trained them to be undependable, unreliable, and every other negative trait he has, they too mimic. Unfortunately, this has left him with an army of failures.

There's a fine line angelic beings must trod. Help can only be given with instructions from the throne, for there's a time to be tested and a time to be shielded from the darts of the enemy. All things work together for good. Fortunately for these young men, they have the blood applied to their lives and God has His hand on their souls. One never knows when an imp from the pit will be passing your way and try your spirit.

As Hans steps back to give room for the intruder to rise and show himself, he notices a large scar on the right side of the demon's face that somehow looks familiar. With a snicker he inquires, "Drate? Oh Drate, surely this can't be true! Things couldn't be going so bad for you since we last met, that you are assigned to harassing these young men!" Hans nudges Kovec and points to Drate, laughing. "And how unfortunate for you that I have been sent here to train my newest officer."

Drate straightens himself and tries to regain some dignity. Clearing his throat, he growls, "How typical of you, Halo Boy, to be totally incorrect." Trying his best to look unaffected by their massive size and obvious strength, he replies, "No, I'm not here on any assignment. I was simply passing by and thought I'd see what all the noise was about. I happen to be on my way to a summit meeting with very important news. Not that it is any of your business." Like his master, Drate couldn't tell the truth if his worthless life depended on it.

"Oh, so they've promoted you to a '**messenger**' now?" Kovec and Hans both continue to laugh uncontrollably. They never dreamed they'd have so much fun when they started out on this tour.

His plans for a little excitement have been defeated, and now being subjected to further humiliation, he snaps at the two who are spoiling his fun. "You wouldn't understand. I'm in charge of a very important project that can only be entrusted to '**me**'." He's grasping for straws now. Poor Drate, he thinks he always has to have the last word.

Drate's anger is very obvious; he's turning a brilliant shade of red.

"Oh, I'm sure you are Drate." Hans is continuing to push Drate's button.

Drate babbles on as though no one were talking but him. "You're making me late. So, if you don't have anything else that you'd like to discuss, then I'll be on my way. This sentimental journey stuff is not my thing." Drate dashes away without even a

Warning. This Is A Test. This Is Only A Test.

glance over his shoulder as the two warriors laugh themselves to tears.

Drate figures that before he gets into any more trouble, and this job gets botched, he'd better get back to the Arrington's house and check in on Mitch and, of course, 'Gunther.' If he lets this simple job go bad he can kiss his promotion goodbye. Making good use of his time, the next few hours before day light will be spent bothering Mitch in his semi-state of sleep. Tonight, Mitch will have some of the most vivid dreams he's ever had.

At the age of five, Mitch was bitten by a stray dog. His father, and the sheriff, tracked down, cornered, and killed the dog. After the dog was submitted for tests, and it was proven to be rabid, Mitch had to undergo a series of extremely painful shots, consisting of one shot a day, for four weeks. Half of the vaccine was administered into the muscle, the other half directly into the bite itself. Since that traumatic incident, dogs have not been his favorite thing. Drate knows this and isn't at all apprehensive about using this piece of information, as well as anything else he knows to really send him into orbit. The first thing an over-enthusiastic imp learns when he's being trained for combat with mortals, is to use every area of their past against them. Lucifer and his co-horts are well aware of everything each human has done and the fact that humans have a difficult time forgiving themselves, makes their past the obvious tool to use against them.

Tossing and turning, Mitch is trying his best to get away from that monstrous dog with the enormous fangs. Growling and barking, the dog appeared to be one huge mouth full of extremely large, razor sharp teeth.

Drate sits back and enjoys the look of fear, and helplessness on Mitch's face. **"Ah, is the little doggy bothering the big man?"** He can't control the screams of laughter. Not that he tries in the slightest.

Running, running, telling himself to run faster, crying for help, but no words come out of his mouth. There isn't any air to breathe. The faster he runs, the slower he seems to be going. Constantly looking back over his shoulder, he can see the dog is rapidly gaining ground. Mitch has worked himself into a sweat. He can feel the dog's hot, humid breath saturating the back of his neck. The dog's powerful bark shakes the very ground beneath Mitch's feet. His thrashing becomes more intense.

The dream ends abruptly and turns to a different setting. The look of fear on his face is replaced with sheer horror.

Drate continues to jeer and make snide comments. "This is really gonna be good." He is having a grand time. Knowing how close Mitch is to his family, he knows this will be a great spot to work on. "These mortals have so many weaknesses that it makes it's almost too easy to torment them." Drate gives himself too much credit.

As the dream unfolds in Mitch's mind, he can see his family trapped in a burning automobile, but he can't make his feet move. His struggling only

Warning. This Is A Test. This Is Only A Test.

seems to make matters worse. He can see no apparent reason for his feet not wanting to move. Frustration turns to fear. His mouth is dry, his palms are wet, and breathing is becoming more difficult. He then notices Chase and Nicole both in the back seat of the car, peering out of the window, with a look of horror on their faces. His heart lodges in his throat, and every inch of his body begins to tremble as helplessness chokes the air from his lungs.

Their pleading little voices sound very faint.
"D-a-d-d-y, h-e-l-p, h-e-l-p!" Their pleas send cold chills over his body. He begins to cry, still struggling to move. Standing only a few yards from his dying family, he is feeling completely helpless.

"Oh, babies, get out of the car! Get out of the car!" He screams, but his words seemingly fall at his feet.

He can now see Victoria as the flames engulf her beautiful face. Her head turns away, trying to escape the flames that are leaping up at her. It now seems as though she is looking straight at him. Her eyes appear to ask the question, "Why? Why don't you help us?"

"Victoria, get out! Get the children and get out!" He can see them as they are totally taken over by the inferno of flames. His heart refuses to beat, his life has just been taken from him, and he is defenseless to do anything about it.

The bed covers are completely in disarray. His thrashing is becoming more and more violent.

Struggling in his dream to get his feet free, he loses his balance and falls twisting his leg. His facial expression leaves no doubt that he's in excruciating pain; he's definitely broken his leg.

The cheering section gets louder with each second, as Drate enjoys a good action thriller. This is one of the best he's seen. "So what are ya' gonna do about this, Mr. Mechanic?"

The screams coming from the charred automobile turn to silence as tears flow down his face. Out of desperation he manages to whisper, **"God, help me!"** He struggles to wake himself up.

Gunther is there with help, nudging Mitch, stroking his mind with peace, and comfort.

Covered in perspiration and tangled bed covers, he's finally back to reality. Gasping for air, his body jolts, his hand grabs his chest, and he sits straight up in the bed. Realizing he's only been dreaming, he feels his racing heart slowly returning to normal.

"Thank God it was just a dream!" Mitch says, relieved beyond words.

"Drate, ole boy, you have stepped over the line!" Gunther warns. "I strongly suggest you find somewhere else to play your mind games. The show is over!"

With his nose in the air, he tries justifying his insidious sense of what's fair. "Oh now, don't get bent out of shape. There's no harm done." Drate cackles, thinking he's gotten away with his unscrupulous deed. "It's all part of the plan." Drate doesn't know how close he's come to being tossed a couple of light years into space. "You don't worry about me. I know what I'm doing. Maybe you should

Warning. This Is A Test. This Is Only A Test.

take your own advice." He hisses, feeling a sense of power and accomplishment.

Victoria, just as exhausted, is awakened by the vigorous commotion on the opposite side of the bed. She raises up to see why he's up **again**, and asks, "Are you okay?" She rubs her tired eyes. "I don't think you've gotten any rest."

"**Rest**, no. I don't think rest and I crossed paths at all!" He says exhausted.

Across the room, the clock sounds its alarm. Tossing the covers back, Mitch announces, "I'm ready to get up, even if it weren't time," he says as he slaps the button on top of the alarm clock, silencing its offensive noise.

Six a.m. isn't too early for the Arringtons this morning. This has been one unpleasant night, and getting up is much better than fighting in your dreams all night.

Victoria feels like she's been in bed with a wrestling team all night. Her spirit tells her they've been invaded by something sinister. She's been expecting it; the good thing is she knows what to do about trouble such as this - **PRAY.**

Mitch climbs into the shower, and tries desperately to forget those horrifying dreams. The fact that they were so real makes forgetting harder. Unfortunately, soap and water can't wash away the haunting feeling he has. The dreams are continuing to replay themselves in his mind. The sound of the dog's barking, the sight of the incinerating flames as they devour his family, run rampant in his thoughts. Just as he felt so helpless all night with the dreams, he is now being subjected to the instant replays. Try though he may he can't seem to shake this force of Despair that has his claws in him.

Victoria slowly makes her way to the kitchen for coffee and some hot breakfast. When the coffee pot finishes with it's spitting and sputtering, she pours two steaming cups and takes one in to Mitch. "Here, Babe, your breakfast is almost ready," she says as she hands him his cup.

He jumps when the door opens. "Oh, you scared me! I didn't hear you coming." He realizes how silly this whole thing is. A grown man scared by a dream. "Thanks." Mitch reaches for his wife and gives her a big hug. He likes the way she giggles when he teases her. "I'm sorry if my tossing kept you awake all night." He tries to shake loose of the vise like grip that has him so jumpy.

Smiling that beauty queen smile, she lingers briefly in his warm embrace. "Come on Mitch, your breakfast is ready." She leaves him to finish getting ready for work.

In the breakfast nook, as the couple enjoys their breakfast together, the conversation goes directly to the night's dreams. "I'm really glad that dreams aren't real! That dog in my dream last night was big enough to eat the tires off a tractor," he says jokingly.

Warning. This Is A Test. This Is Only A Test.

"I've told you about eating hot dogs so late." She pokes his arm and smiles on her way to the kitchen for more coffee.

He spins around in his chair. "Don't even kid about that. You know how much I like hot dogs!" He smiles, but at the same time he can still see every vivid detail of the night's dreams in his mind.

"I was only joking." A wide smile covers her face.

His tone becomes serious, he raises his eye brows, and shakes his finger at Victoria. "If I really thought my dream last night had anything **at all** to do with eating hot dogs, you could be sure I'd never eat another one as long as I live!" He hasn't mentioned anything about the second dream and he isn't planning on it either.

Filling their cups with fresh coffee, she rejoins him back at the table. "Come on, finish your breakfast. You have to get to work." Spreading her favorite peach preserves on her toast she adds, "you do realize that we have been targeted by the enemy, and we are under direct attack? I felt it when it came in our room last night. We need to stay in a constant state of prayer." Her words conveyed faith, but her facial expression told of her merited concern.

Mitch knows better than anyone of the presence of the enemy. "Let's make sure we plead the Blood of Jesus, and ask for God's will to be done before we even get out of the house this morning!"

After breakfast, the Arringtons have their usual time of prayer together before they start their day. They know the danger of going out into the world unprotected. You just don't go out without a fresh coat of polish on your armor. Too many everyday mishaps can cause you to lose what victory you have, and making sure your lamp is full of oil before you go out into a storm is only smart. Today more than ever they choose their words carefully. They don't want to speak anything negative, giving the enemy any more ammunition.

After prayer, Mitch gets his lunch and his jacket. "I'll call you at noon to see how things are going. If you need me, you call." Mitch leans down to kiss his petite wife goodbye.

"You take care of yourself. We have God on our side, and there's nothing that will happen to us that he hasn't already approved." Her smile reassures him she will be okay.

2 Corinthians 4:7-9

7   But we have this treasure in earthen vessels, that the excellency of the power may be of God, and not of us.

8   We are troubled on every side, yet not distressed; we are perplexed, but not in despair;

9   Persecuted, but not forsaken; cast down, but not destroyed;
(KJV)

Warning. This Is A Test. This Is Only A Test.

A Call To Prayer

3

Lying back in the big oak tree outside the Arrington's bedroom window, doing what he does best, nothing, Drake is shaken by the sound of praying and comes to himself. He's fallen asleep on the job, **again**. He covers his big hairy ears and begins to curse. "I'd rather be sent out to the most boring assignment or to the most dangerous mission as to be around these **praying, singing Christians**." His shouting can be heard for miles around. "Just the sound of their voices short circuits my system." He hears Mitch and Victoria pleading the Blood of Jesus. "I can't stand hearing that **Name**." He tosses his head back and screeches. "It's the ultimate goal, the sworn duty, of every evil minded imp, demon, deva, and lord of darkness to have these pesky Christians wiped completely off the face of the earth. Lucifer demands it." He stops, only to gasp for air. "When the demise of the entire Christian population is accomplished, and - it - shall - be - soon, our lord and great ruler, Lucifer, will take charge of the earth and we will be in complete and utter control." He finishes his frothy sermon, steps off his soap box, and tries to calm himself. He really works himself into a frenzy when he talks about the Christians.

Mitch hurries off to the shop, after prayer, followed by Drate, who's followed by Gunther. Continuing to meditate on the thought he'd gotten during the morning prayer time, he marvels at how good God is to reassure His people that He will never leave us nor forsake us. After a night like last night, it is comforting to know that there is hope. The drive to the shop takes about twenty minutes. Mitch has an uneasy feeling in his spirit, something just isn't quite right, but he can't seem to put his finger on it. Is it the dreams still haunting him? Is it the demonic force that he and Victoria fought all night? He is certain there is something going on, and the only thing he's ever known to do at a time like this is to praise and create an atmosphere of worship. Starting with his favorite songs, and working his way down the list, Mitch leans back and begins to sing to his hearts' content.

Warning. This Is A Test. This Is Only A Test.

God's Word says, 'He inhabits the praises of His people.'

Drate isn't going to follow too closely, but it has nothing to do with the fact that Mitch Arrington can't carry a tune. He just can't handle the power that praise brings. Keeping his distance from Gunther, and an eye out for any other opposition, he goes over his grand plan once more before he actually activates the murderous scheme. He's had imps following Mitch, watching his every move for several days, and laying plans to trap him. What better place for a deadly accident than the Shepherd County Garage, with all it's equipment, chemicals, and hazardous activities, laid out at Drate's feet.

Finally at the shop, Drate is free to go about his business. With a mischievous gleam in his eyes, and a skip in his stride, he waltzes around the shop. Feeling invincible, he rehearses his plan out loud hoping Gunther will hear. "Yep, that poor fella', Mitch, won't have a chance. Today is his lucky day." Drate spots the trailer with the track hoe on it that his imps overheard two men talking about yesterday. "We're just gonna see about this God he boasts so much about. If he thought last night was bad, wait until he sees what I have planned for him today! I'm finished with the dreams and make believe, today's gonna be the real thing." Drate's showing his true colors, his more natural bloodthirsty side. "You just don't mess with Drate, the future lord of darkness."

He pauses for effect, as he looks around trying to spot Gunther.

Gunther is doing his best to follow orders, but it's extremely difficult to listen to blasphemous words about his Lord. The enemy knows the angelic hosts only move when they are given orders from the Throne, unlike their evil lot, who are deliberately vile, characteristically vicious, fiendishly depraved, and have no conscience, or guide.

"Yep, it's a well known fact, when I'm given a job to do, I will accomplish the task. No holds barred, just me and my assigned target. That's the way I like it. When I get finished with this Mitch fella', he won't know what hit him." He laughs a belly laugh.

Arrogant must have been his Father's name, and Pride surely was his Mother's.

Gunther has found himself a vantage point outside the garage, and is standing watch. Drate is still parading around boasting about what he's going to do. Unfortunately, he's dreaming again.

Gunther wants a chance to teach Drate a lesson. "Lord if you would just give me the word, I will make short work of this boasting, outlandish, barbarian." He sees too often the pain and heartache caused by these demonic misfits, and the disrespectful way they treat the children of the Most High. If it wasn't for the reverence this Heavenly Warrior has for his Lord, Drate would have been history, eons ago.

Warning. This Is A Test. This Is Only A Test.

At the Arrington's modest home, there's an urgency in the air. Kreig knows what's coming and tugs at Victoria's heart strings. Even though she's already had her morning prayer time, she checks on the children at play in their rooms and returns to her bedroom to kneel and pray. After a night like last night, she is prepared for an attack. She is no stranger to this urgency that she is feeling. Several times in the past she's received confirmation on things she's prayed about.

When she and Mitch were first married, she was at home, alone, trying to get things organized at their apartment. While she worked, she began to sing, the singing turned to mourning, and then into a heart wrenching cry. The need to get on her knees was overwhelming; she fell to the floor, and began to plead the blood of Jesus. Her sister came to mind as clearly as if she were standing in front of her.

Later that evening, she received a phone call from her sister, Cricket. "It was horrible." Cricket began to relay the chilling ordeal she'd gone through. "There I stood alone with a mugger in the parking lot at the bank. He had a gun to my head and was telling me he was going to kill me if I didn't cooperate. Then God sent a miracle. Before I had time to give him my purse, a car came around the corner. He panicked and ran. There have been two other people robbed in the past month and one was badly beaten. I know God spared me." Her voice shook just talking about it.

Victoria knows why the car drove by at that exact time her sister was getting off work and was being confronted by a mugger. She'd prayed, at the prompting of God, and He had sent a miracle her way.

In the spring, two years ago, as Victoria went about her daily chores, she was singing and worshipping as she normally did. She had taken a peek in at her one year old daughter, Nicole, who was napping, when she felt compelled to check on Chase, her three year old son, who was at play in the back yard. Stepping out onto the back porch she didn't see Chase. Immediate concern gripped her heart, she sensed something was wrong. "Oh Jesus." She said softly. In the far corner of the yard she spotted a little red shirt hiding behind a tree. She called out to him, but he did not respond. Stepping off the porch she made her way to the tree, and Chase. He stood as though he were spellbound, fascinated with something in front of him. There on the ground only a few feet away, biding it's time, was a rattle snake, coiled, and ready to strike. Her heart felt as though it would stop beating. She had no weapon, or way, to kill the snake, but she had the power of the Name of Jesus. Pointing her hands at the snake she demanded, "In Jesus Name, I command you to be gone." Immediately the snake uncoiled, slithered away, and never looked back. Victoria grabbed Chase up into her arms, "Thank you Jesus for warning me. Oh Chase, Mommy's so proud you're okay." She knows the power prayer has, and the rewards of praying without ceasing.

Warning. This Is A Test. This Is Only A Test.

It seems that every family she knows has been under severe attack lately. This time is different from before. There is something so haunting in the air, something so urgent. Her heart is heavy and the tears seem to gush forth. What is this need? Who is this under attack?

Unaware that the stump of a demon, Grice, has been sent to hinder her prayers, and is at this very moment on a downward spiral directly over her home, she begins praying.

Grice is a second stringer, but then, why would you send a warrior to do a wimp's job? This is a very simple task. All he has to do is distract the Arrington woman for a few minutes while Drate does his dirty deeds.

Kreig fervently stands guard and watches Grice like a hawk. The one thing angelic beings like least of all is having to control their desire to banish any and all spirits of darkness from existence. But they, too, like the pesky mosquito, have their place in the grand design. Their noisome end is near at hand. There is but one Ruler, one King, and one High Priest, **Jesus**.

T he ruler of darkness is once again going to be extremely disappointed. He's met his match in Victoria Arrington. She is well aware of the tricks the enemy uses, and is not easily distracted by the thoughts that try to flood her mind. It may have worked when she was first starting to learn about this prayer business, but now she has experienced for herself, the power brought forth from prayer.

Poking and prodding at her thoughts, Grice tries desperately to distract her praying. "Today's laundry day; you really should go put a load in the washing machine before you start!" He whispers over and over again.

Victoria continues to plead the blood of Jesus, and Kreig continues to stroke her mind with comforting thoughts.

Rubbing his grotesque little hands together, he's sure to get her attention now. "Isn't that Nicole crying?" His squeaky, demented, little voice alone is enough to distract.

Towering over Grice, Kreig interrupts the shriveled, smelly little pest. "Give it up you little runt. You're wasting your time with this one." he chides.

"Are you afraid I'm going to discourage her? You know my cunning power of persuasion is working." Grice sneers, from a safe distance of course. Kreig is about eight times larger than Grice.

Continuing with his vain efforts to discourage this, as he boastfully refers, mere mortal, he tries another approach. "Oh no, you forgot to give Mitch his lunch this morning!" He uses every excuse he can think of, but she's not budging.

"Do yourself a favor flea, and go bother somebody else." Kreig continues to insult Grice.

"You aren't gonna stop me. I have lots more tricks up my sleeve." Grice moves to plan B. "Ah ha, the children are playing in the other room!" Grice is

Warning. This Is A Test. This Is Only A Test.

about to get a little help from the little Arringtons. That's his plan anyway.

Victoria hears the crying and fussing in the other room from where she is praying. She's well aware that the enemy tries to distract her by using any tactic he can find, including her children, and she's not falling for it. She knows that what she is feeling has to be a plea from above to help someone and she isn't going to let them, or herself down. Everything else will have to wait. Immediate and fervent prayer goes up, and the power comes down.

Entering the children's room, Grice is met by two enormous warriors, Jet and Arless. He decides this isn't going to work and backs out of the room without taking his eyes off the two towering masses of intimidation. "Okay, bad idea. Maybe I'll just go and do something else." He mumbles his apology as he's exiting.

The children's room is once again silent and Victoria is free to continue praying.

Poor little Grice is trying desperately to break this lady's concentration, but he just doesn't have the stuff. The devil himself has no power unless God gives it, and his imps have even less power. Not ready just yet to throw in the towel, Grice continues to poke, scream, and torment Victoria in her time of prayer.

Kreig stands near by looking on, nodding his head in disbelief. "How can you even think you are making any progress?" He asks Grice.

Kreig is proud of the dedication and determination in this mortal. He continues to comfort her with words of encouragement. He whispers to her, "So shall they fear the name of the LORD from the West, and his glory from the rising of the sun. When the enemy shall come in like a flood, the **Spirit of the LORD shall** lift up a standard against him."

Job 1:7-8

7 And the LORD said unto Satan, Whence comest thou? Then Satan answered the LORD, and said, From going to and fro in the earth, and from walking up and down in it.

8 And the LORD said unto Satan, Hast thou considered my servant Job, that there is none like him in the earth, a perfect and an upright man, one that feareth God, and escheweth evil?

(KJV)

Warning. This Is A Test. This Is Only A Test.

The Attack

4

Across town at the Shepherd County Garage, business is as usual. Trucks are coming and going, equipment is being loaded onto trailers, and tanks are being pumped full of diesel fuel. The men are getting ready to spend another day repairing pot holes, ruts, and worn out, black top roads. This has already been an unusually, hard winter for this part of Texas, and more of the drizzling, freezing weather is on the way. With the foot of snow that fell in November, and the torrential rains that have been falling this month, the roads are in bad need of repairs.

Out of sight, peering from every nook and cranny, a legion of eager little nasties await their signal to swarm the garage. They've been instructed to create a distraction and work on the men's concentration. Drate has it all planned and everyone knows their job. Mass confusion is the order.

Mitch has spent the first three hours of his day putting a new motor in one of the dump trucks. Pleased that he has done a good job, he is preparing to get to the next job on his list. Clean up in itself, is always a big job.

Above the roar of the machinery, and the every day noises, a plea from a crew member rings out across the garage. "Hey, give us a hand here!" The cry sounds urgent.

As the men are loading an eight ton track hoe onto a trailer, Drate punctures the hydraulic line causing fluid to spray out onto the floor. With one more effort Drate succeeds, causing the line to burst open, and fluid is now pouring out. Something has to be done before the boom swings off the trailer causing the track hoe to tilt too far, and fall to the garage floor.

Drate stands back snickering, pleased with himself for thinking of such an ingenious idea. Completely satisfied with the results of his plans, he shouts, "How 'bout that for a crowd pleaser?" He's hoping Gunther is getting to see the entire show.

As all the men race to help, the track hoe bucket swings off the trailer bed, and causes an imbalance. Drate moves in to give that extra bit of push, leaning on the track hoe from the far side of the trailer as it continues to lean.

Gunther knows this is all part of the master plan, but still finds it difficult to simply stand by and watch.

One of the crewmen yells out a warning, "Heads up Arrington, it's coming off the trailer!" The

Warning. This Is A Test. This Is Only A Test.

men scatter like feathers in the wind. There's nothing they can do now but stand back and watch.

Trying to get out of the way, Mitch loses his footing in the fluid. Slipping, sliding, and arms flailing, he hits the floor with a thud. The real problem was Drate's big clubfoot placed in Mitch's way.

Standing back admiring his handy work, Drate throws his hairy arms in the air, feigning his innocence. "Oh, excuse me! Was my foot in your way?" He gets hours of pleasure out of his sadistic sense of humor.

Everyone scatters and the big mass of metal machinery falls to the ground behind them with a deafening roar.

With their adrenaline rushing, they check to see what damage has been done and make sure all the men are okay. As the dust settles and some sense of calm returns, they discover that one of the men has been trapped under the massive piece of steel. A leg and an arm can be seen protruding from the heap in the middle of the garage floor. Cautiously the men approach the pile of metal crumpled on top of flesh and bone.

Drate signals the legion of demons to get to their duties and cause havoc. Like a swarm of flies at a watermelon party, the imps take flight. With his little imps causing confusion, and spreading fear, it will be easy for his plan to work.

"It's Arrington! He's not moving and he isn't responding to my voice." Roy, one of the truck drivers reports.

The demon, Fear, is crouched on Roy's shoulder, whispering. "He's dead, he can't hear you, and there's nothing you can do for him."

"Get the winch truck !" Corky the shop foreman yells, as the demon Anger, takes a hand full of his brain in his crusty little paw and gives it a twisting squeeze.

"Someone - get - an - ambulance!" Tom, another co-worker orders, as Panic and Confusion dig their fiendish claws into the base of his skull.

The shop looks like an ant hill on a busy summer afternoon. Everyone's trying to find a way to help, but there seems to be more harm being done than good. Tempers are flaring, Fear is causing conflicts, thoughts are being stolen from their minds, and everything is in total chaos. Their hearts are pounding as Fear grips them; this is one of theirs, and they are afraid. On the shoulder of every man is a dripping, oozing imp, with fingernails like meat hooks imbedded into their necks, as they inject the drugs of Fear, Anger, and Confusion. As the imps' bloodthirsty appetites are being quenched, the air is filled with cackling and demonic laughter.

The screeching and wailing of the imps sounds more like a herd of fighting wild pigs. They can't even get along with themselves, when they're supposedly on the same side. Demons just know how to hate. It's nothing personal.

The demon Deceiver, is stroking Drate's ego with fabricated words. "Oh Lord Drate, Tinga will be greatly pleased. You have been victorious this day."

Warning. This Is A Test. This Is Only A Test.

Filled with false satisfaction, he puffs his chest out, and struts around the garage. **"Gott-cha!"** Drate shouts. **"Who - says - you - Christians - are - so - tough?"** There will be no stopping Drate now, as far as he is concerned, he is what makes the sun rise, and set.

The demon Deceiver continues to exalt Drate, "Stay and see the end of this matter. You deserve to hear, with your own ears, your enemy declare you the Victor in this battle."

As his head swells to mammoth proportions, he announces to the world. "Yes, I do deserve to see the look on Gunther's face when he has to tuck his tail and admit my cunning abilities far exceed his simple minded ways."

Drate has always gotten a thrill out of inflicting pain, and today is even better in his eyes. Spotting Gunther, he raises his hands to indicate a triumphant win, for this is actually two victories in one. Mitch is his assignment, and defeating Gunther, his long time enemy, is just an added bonus.

Gunther stands by, anxiously, waiting for orders. At the slightest signal he is ready to make a quick work of this gutless wonder. But no signal comes. His hands are tied, **for now**.

Two of the men race across the yard to get the winch truck. The dose of confusion they've been given is working its' work.

"Where's - that - truck?" One man demands. The demon Rage, is having himself a busy day.

"It was parked right here the last time I saw it!" Tempers flare, Fear is launching an all out attack.

"There it is behind the fork lift."

"Well, who put it there?"

The plague of imps are spreading their infectious poison to as many minds as they possibly can, and enjoying every minute of it.

To those standing by waiting for the winch truck to get into position, it seems like an eternity. Bickering starts, and bad attitudes begin to show their faces.

Knowing the cold cement floor beneath Mitch won't help his condition, several of his co-workers have gotten jackets to cover his motionless body. They know Arrington is a God-fearing man, and are breathing a prayer for him.

The little imps begin to squirm. They don't like prayer in any form. One by one the mass of bat like imps disappear into the sky. They've done all they've been ordered to do, no one said they had to hang around and be subjected to 'praying'. Going that extra mile isn't part of the deal, and loyalty to the cause is not one of their attributes.

As the truck pulls around and the winch is hooked up, the men that are on the floor trying to be of some comfort move back, in hopes this will be the answer to their problems. No one is really sure if the winch will lift this machine.

The ambulance can be heard in the distance as it races to the aid of the first accident of the day. With the majority of the demons gone, some of the men feel more free to think and can operate a little

Warning. This Is A Test. This Is Only A Test.

clearer. A few of the men step outside to direct the ambulance.

Inside the garage, the signals are given to the driver of the winch truck, and the winch motor begins to clank and grind.

"Easy now, easy." Blake, the shop welder signals to the driver. "It's coming, but take it slow."

The ambulance arrives about the time the men are attempting to pull Mitch from under the machinery. The team leaps from the ambulance, throws open the rear doors, and unloads what seems to be a mini hospital with crash carts, I. V. bottles, backboards, neck braces, and radio equipment. Like a choreographed performance that has been rehearsed over and over, the technicians go to their jobs. Everyone knows what to do, but time is slipping away.

The winch has managed to lift the track hoe up several feet. As if they are moving an explosive device set to go off at the slightest movement, these men pull the body out from under the fallen mass. No one is sure how long he's been under the weight of the machine, but it seems like an eternity. Fortunately for Mitch, the winch is sturdy enough to do the job. Finally clear, they order the winch to lay the crumpled, metal death trap, down again. They don't need another accident.

The shock of what is happening hasn't quite hit the men yet. As they stand looking on, the team of dedicated technicians work feverishly to save this man's life.

The men from the shop seem to fade into the back ground. Like mannequins in a department store window, they silently look on. They can hear the E. M. T. Crew talking, but it is like they are dreaming. Reality is slowly setting in.

Corky, Roy, Tom, and some of the other men are standing back taking it all in.

Corky numbly comments, "We haven't had a serious accident here since I've been at this garage." He hangs his head.

"Arrington was such a nice fella' to work with." Roy says, as though he thinks Mitch isn't going to make it.

"He's gonna be okay! We have to believe he's gonna be okay." Corky sounds like he's still trying to convince himself. He stands silently staring at the lifeless body. This has hit him hard.

From his vantage point overhead, Drate scolds the paramedics. "Don't waste your time," he begins to snicker, " he's history. I saw to that."

Gunther is set on go. He is so ready to make 'Drate' history. All he needs is a slight jester from above, permitting him to intervene. It is hard to stand by and do nothing. But orders are orders, and he's come to know that God's way is always best.

The hospital has been contacted and is ready for information. "Do you have the vitals ready, crew one?" Doctor Jeffreys, asks.

"I have a pulse of twelve, and a B. P. of fifty over thirty. We're gonna need care flight here A.S.A.P.. This man is critical." Crew one replies.

Warning. This Is A Test. This Is Only A Test.

"How is his breathing?" Doctor Jeffreys is collecting information to prescribe a plan of action.

"Labored and shallow." The crew knows it doesn't look good, but that isn't hindering them from doing all they know to do to save this man's life.

"Care flight's on it's way. Standby." Doctor Jeffreys sets things in motion from his end making the necessary arrangements to receive the patient.

The medic crew keeps in constant contact with the hospital until the Care Flight transport crew arrives. The E. M. T. Crew works to get him ready to go aboard the helicopter. Everyone knows it is bad, but if anyone knows how bad it really is, they aren't saying.

Within minutes the Care Flight Helicopter is overhead, circling the building, looking for the best place to land.

Crew one shields Mitch's body from blowing debris. The shop's crew steps out of the door way of the garage, covering their faces from the dust storm. As the helicopter slowly lowers to the ground, some fifty feet away, a cloud of dust rises up into the blue cloud covered sky, dimming the suns glare. The medic crew rushes out past the group of men, to load Mitch for transporting.

Corky realizes that the Road Commissioner, Vernon Henderson, hasn't been told what's happened, and Mrs. Arrington doesn't know yet! Someone needs to call them both. Unfortunately, the job falls in his lap. As he picks up the phone receiver in the office, away from the noise, a call comes in on the other line. He answers the incoming call, delaying the task he is dreading. "Hello, District Four, this is Corky." He replies simply out of habit. His mind is not on business.

"Corky, this is Vern. **What - is - going - on over - there**?" He sounds anxious. "I was with Sheriff Roland when the call to dispatch came over the radio for an ambulance to be sent out to the shop. We were out on County Road 4322, at the north edge of the town, and I've been trying to reach you for almost half an hour." There's a short pause. "Corky, are you there?" Vern has no idea the seriousness of this call.

"There's been an accident, Vern." He pauses to swallow. "Arringtons been hurt, he's hurt pretty bad." Corky's distraught state is immediately evident.

"What's happened?" The level of stress Vern is under has just been escalated by fifty percent.

"The track hoe that we were loading to go out to the job on County Road 421 somehow sprung a leak in the hydraulic line. The men gave a warning that the bucket was swinging off center, and then the track hoe fell off the trailer, trapping Arrington under it." Corky is feeling somewhat responsible, and blaming himself. After all he was in charge.

"I'm on my way there now. Has his wife been called?" Vern's words are blunt and his tone intense.

"No, not yet. I was about to call you when the phone rang. The Care Flight is about to leave here now, so you may want to go on to the hospital from there. It'll save you time. Everything is under control here." From the office window he watches the procedures.

Warning. This Is A Test. This Is Only A Test.

"Okay, I'm gonna call his wife and let her know what's happened." This is the part of his job Vern dislikes the most.

"Thanks boss, I really wasn't looking forward to making that call." The tears welling up in Corky's eye's are causing him to choke up.

"Cork, you know that this isn't your fault, don't be blaming yourself." Vern could hear the sound of guilt in his voice. He knows how soft hearted Corky is.

"Thanks boss, I better get the men back to work, we are getting behind." After hanging up the phone, he takes a minute to calm down and wipe the tears from his dust covered cheeks.

Back out in the shop bay, the medics rush Mitch out to the helicopter to make the trip across the county to the hospital. Unseen by mortal eyes is the ever faithful Gunther. He is in place and ready to go. As the helicopter takes off, everyone's left with a feeling of emptiness. As the demon's drugs completely wear off, the men are able to think clearly and the bone chilling truth hits the men - **HARD**.

Corky rejoins the crowd of men still obviously shaken up by this horrendous tragedy. "Okay guys, listen up. There's nothing else we can do. Let the doctor's take it from here. Vern is on his way to the hospital now, so I'll keep you posted on any news that comes in. Let's just get back to work."

Luke 8:24 And they came to him, and awoke him, saying, Master, master, we perish. Then he arose, and rebuked the wind and the raging of the water: and they ceased, and there was a calm.
(KJV)

Warning. This Is A Test. This Is Only A Test.

The Calm Before The Storm

5

In the bedroom of the Arrington's modest home, a sweet peace comes over the room and Victoria knows her prayers are being heard and the answer is on it's way.

Kreig continues to reassure Victoria that God is in control.

Grice is almost out of energy and can't take this praying any longer; he is out of here. Using what energy he has left, he bolts to the sky, and heads home, mumbling to himself. "How do they do it? I gave it my best stuff and she still prays! Drate is going to be furious. Odds are, Tinga will never give me another assignment." Discourage was what he'd been sent to do to Victoria Arrington. As is usually the case for Grice, he ends up doing a great job of discouraging himself.

The pressure she has been battling lifts, and in it's place, comes a reassuring feeling that somehow all is well. Lingering in the sweet presence of the Lord for a little longer, she's reminded of the words of the old song, "I Know The Lord Will Make A Way Somehow."

At the other end of the house, the phone begins to ring. She glances at the clock on the table across from her and realizes she's been praying for over an hour. It seems like minutes. She pulls herself up off the floor, and races to get the phone. She's hoping it's Mitch. She wants to tell him about the awesome prayer meeting she's just had.

D rate, feeling pretty proud of himself, spins and turns to streak across the sky. He has good news to report. Gesturing in Gunther's direction, Drate dusts his hands off, implying another dirty Christian out of the way. Muttering to himself, he hurries back to Tinga. He is sure to be promoted after this. Patting himself on the back, he goes over the events once more. How pleased he seems, having won this victory today. This little family has been a thorn in his side for some time now. Every time he's tried to promote the dark side's agenda in this dinky little town, these Christians show up and start telling that story about, **"a better way."** Every time he is convinced they are down for the count, someone pulls them through with prayer. Obviously, this time is different. Becoming so outraged about the christians, he begins talking to himself, out loud. "Ha, we have the better way. Better for us that they are all gone and we take over, with me in charge. It's about time I am recognized for my

Warning. This Is A Test. This Is Only A Test.

many talents." He rambles on the entire trip, about how deserving he is, too bad no one else is listening, or cares.

As he glides in on wings of haughtiness, into the room full of underlings, they bow and show reverence to his office, but more so to **his bad temper**. They know it wouldn't take anything more than a slight flick of his wrist to send each of them out into orbit. This adds another inch to his stature. He has no sense of team play. He is for himself, and himself only. The top position is his ultimate goal, and he has no time, or sympathy, for anyone or anything. Nearing the entrance to his superior's chamber, Tinga's private lair, he straightens his shoulders and barks, "**Drate to see Tinga. Announce me, I have urgent news!**"

The little shriveled up guard announces him. "Master, Drate is here with news."

Drate is ushered into the lair he lusts after for his own. Confident this victory will be the key to his acquiring this position, he goes in acting like he owns the place.

Victoria reaches the phone, picks up the receiver, and tossing her head back to get the hair out of her face. "Hello." There is no response, so she again, with a question in her voice, says, "Hello?"

Kreig is at Victoria's side making sure she has a constant flow of support and encouragement. With his sword drawn he waits for the demon Fear and Discouragement to show their ugly faces.

"Mrs. Arrington?" A reluctant voice asks.

"Yes, this is Mrs. Arrington." She answers. She's heard this voice somewhere before, but where?

"Mrs. Arrington, this is Vern Henderson. I hope I haven't called at a bad time!" His palms are sweaty, his mouth is as dry as a stretch of West Texas highway, and his chest is aching. He doesn't want to have to say the words he knows he is about to say. No amount of motivational training, or gung-ho career management course prepares a person for times like this.

"Oh hello, Mr. Henderson, my husband isn't home. He's working at the garage today." She's assuming he's calling for her husband.

"Yes, he is at the shop, but, well, I don't know any other way to say this but to just come right out and say it." Stumbling for words he decides to take the direct approach.

"You don't know how to say what?" Her voice takes an immediate turn from pleasant, to curious. "What's happened? What do you mean?"

Kreig spots the demonic forces in the distance.

He knows his place and intends to keep a keen eye on these renegades.

As they draw near, they can be heard bragging and boasting about their plans for the Arrington lady. "Too bad about her poor husband being crushed under that big machine." Fear throws his head back, and laughs a demonic laugh.

The phone line is silent. Vern is trying to think of another way to put this. Sitting in his diesel extended cab truck, across from the Sheriff's office,

Warning. This Is A Test. This Is Only A Test.

his stomach begins to knot up, he wishes he were somewhere else today. "I'm afraid there's been an accident." As the words go out of his mouth, he realizes how blunt that statement sounds. Pounding his fist into the seat cushion next to him, he scolds himself for not thinking of an easier way of breaking the news to her.

Discouragement slithers up close to Victoria's side and hisses, "He's probably dead. All the praying in the world can't bring him back now."

Kreig flexes his muscles and moves in even closer to Victoria.

"Hey guy, this is our job. We won't mess with you, and you leave us alone!" Fear criticizes.

"You stay on your side of the line and everything will be fine. I'm not leaving her for one second." Kreig growls and flashes his sword in their faces.

"Accident?" Victoria's soft voice questions. It's all too hard to believe. She's sure she must have misunderstood. This just can't be happening! "What kind of an accident, and where is Mitch?"

"I'm so sorry Mrs. Arrington. I called as soon as I found out." His stomach knots are getting tighter.

"Where is he?" She asks again, as her heart slows down to a turtles pace.

Kreig, Fear, and Discouragement stand toe to toe, each refusing to give an inch.

"Well, he's on his way to County Memorial Hospital now. If you'd like, Mrs. Arrington, I am about to leave to go by and see how things are. I'd be glad to come by and give you a lift."

"No, no, thank you. That won't be necessary. I have my car, but thank you for calling. I really need to be going." Deciding it's no misunderstanding, and she has heard correctly, she is in a rush to get off the phone and to the hospital. Her heart begins to pound, and her mind is racing.

Fear and Discouragement continue to jab and poke at her thoughts. It's their plan to get her so distraught that she'll forget the prayer meeting, and the reassurance she's received.

"I'm really sorry I don't have any further news for you. All I know at this point is that he's been hurt." Trying so hard to correct his blunder he continues to trip over his own words.

"Thank you for calling. I'd like to leave now and go see about Mitch." She hangs up the phone.

The phone line is silent. Vernon Henderson sits holding the receiver, wishing he'd not had to be the bearer of such news.

Victoria stops for a brief moment to recall the feeling she'd had, and the reason she'd prayed earlier. The song rang in her ear once more, "I Know The Lord Will Make A Way Somehow." Fighting back Fears, tears, and Anger, she knows what she has to do.

Fear and Discouragement have just lost their battle. But they continue to hang around hoping for another open door.

With Kreig, Arless, and Jet leading the way, she quickly, and calmly gathers the children and drives them to her parent's house, explaining that she has to go to town and see someone at the hospital. All

Warning. This Is A Test. This Is Only A Test.

the while breathing a prayer for Mitch, binding devils, and loosing God's spirit as she goes. When the praying begins, Fear, and Discouragement take off like scalded dogs. With every muscle in her body tense, chin quivering and her heart pounding, she tries to hold her composure. Just a few more miles and she'll drop the children off at her parent's house.

As they come around the corner her mother is working out in the yard, and meets her at the drive. The children bail out of the car almost before it comes to a complete stop. "Grandma, we get to stay for a while. Where's Pa?" They race across the yard and jump onto the pile of freshly raked leaves, scattering them about.

Jet and Arless find stations and set up watch over the children.

"Well, Victoria, I wasn't expecting to see you and the children today. What a nice surprise." Her mother, Ruby Miller, said with a smile. She notices the look on her daughter's face and knows this isn't a visit. She and her daughter share a lot of the same mannerisms. She's reading her daughter's face like a book. "Victoria, what's the matter?" Ruby knows it has to be fairly serious for her daughter to be this disturbed. She places her hand on Victoria's shoulder, "Hun, you're shaking like a leaf!"

Kreig compels her to open up, and let some of the pressure off.

"Mom, there's been an accident, and Mitch is at the hospital. The children don't know. I'll let you know more as soon as I find out what's going on."

She breaks down into a shaking, sobbing, river of tears.

Ruby opens the car door and pulls Victoria close to her. "Oh Baby, I am so sorry. You go ahead and I'll take care of the children. Don't you worry about them one bit."

She straightens up and looks at her Mother, as she wipes away her tears, and one corner of her mouth curls, depicting a weak smile. "I've gotta go. Pray Mom, pray." With that said, she is gone.

Psalms 6:9-10

9 The LORD hath heard my supplication; the LORD will receive my prayer.

10 Let all mine enemies be ashamed and sore vexed: let them return and be ashamed suddenly.

(KJV)

Warning. This Is A Test. This Is Only A Test.

Plan B

6

"Enter, Drate," says a deep gurgling voice. Tinga hisses, as he slouches back in his seat, and folds his muscular arms. He's anxious to hear the spectacular story Drate has to tell about the great victory he's just won.

Drate glides in on a cloud of self-righteousness, glowing with glee at the ease in which 'he's' taken care of that mortal speck of dirt, Arrington. "Tinga, you're looking well, and the news of victory I bring to your ears will make you feel even better." He carries such a high opinion of himself, he can't imagine everyone not feeling the same way.

With a coldness in his black eyes, that bears a startling resemblance to a hungry shark, Tinga casually rises to his feet, and then lets out a roar for all to hear. "Silence, you blabbering idiot. I haven't asked you to speak, nor do I wish to hear your version of how you put a end to this tiny little problem."

Motioning to the corner of the room with his one massive crusty hand, out comes the dwarfed, wrinkled, and cowardly Grice. "Tell Drate, my little one, how things went at the Arrington's today." Tinga slowly resumes his original position in his majestic throne.

Drate's shocked at the manner in which he is being treated. After all, he's just won a great battle. He expects a heroes' welcome, and he is scolded like a deserter. "But your Eminence----!" He tries to explain. After all he's done, he has to make Tinga understand his side.

Tinga picks up his sword, places the fine, sharp, point directly on Drate's throat and dares him to utter another word. "Silence! I'll have you terminated if you speak out again." He lowers the blade and nods to Grice. "Continue, little one. Tell Drate what you have told me of this great victory." Tinga leans back in his chair, and waits to see the look on Drate's face when he hears the news Grice has to share.

With every inch of his puny little body shivering, he inches his way forward, out into the open. "Well, Sir," his voice quivers, he takes another deep breath, swallows, and tries to start again, "as I told you before, Sir, the Arrington woman continued to pray, despite my best efforts to distract her. I did just as Drate ordered me, but we failed." Grice flinched as if he were about to be hit.

Drate swirls around, faces Grice, and with eyes of blue fire, looks his accuser straight in the eyes.

Warning. This Is A Test. This Is Only A Test.

"You accuse me of failure?" He raises his hand to hit Grice.

Grice falls to the floor and crawls to Tinga's side.

Patting Grice on the head, a smirk comes across Tinga's face. "So, Drate, what were you about to say? Something about making me feel even better?" His head turns ever so slowly until his eyes rest on the infamous Drate standing in the middle of the room, all alone.

Being his usual arrogant self, Drate barks back to Tinga and declares, " I have not failed," waving his arms around to exaggerate his point. He is sinking fast, but he's not smart enough to know it. "The job has been done, and done right." He stubbornly persists. Pointing to Grice and sneering, "This poor excuse of an underling was only to distract her praying. Either her prayers were not heard, or I overpowered those prayers with my superior cunning." His chest inflates with self glorification. "So what if the woman prays! She obviously failed; it was not me." He continues to parade around the room. He's aware that a moving target is harder to hit, and Tinga is still wielding his sword. "Her husband is in the hospital, as - we - speak." His tone enraged Tinga. He's forgotten for a moment who he is addressing.

Having heard all of the excuses and lies he cares to listen to, he firmly reminds Drate of his orders. "Your job was not to put him in the hospital." Tinga rises from his chair and confronts Drate, nose to nose. "The orders were to **KILL** the mortal. **Why -**

is - he - still - alive? Your job was to get rid of the Arrington man, and put fear in the remaining Christians. This praying - **MUST - STOP**!" Tinga is demanding an explanation and he is demanding it **NOW**. "**I want results not excuses**."

They are both standing nose to nose as if they are having a debate, and the winner is to out shout the other. The only thing that keeps Tinga from simply turning Drate into a pile of dust is the fact that he is the only one available to do the job with any hope of getting it done in this century. Much more of this obstinate, disrespectful muttering, and he'll forget that he needs Drate and handle the task himself.

Infuriated, Tinga backs away, and issues new orders. "Go, now, and bring me word of the end of this wart of a man. I want him done away with, **NOW**!!" Tinga's voice can be heard outside the deserted town they've taken over and rings out for miles. "If you fail to accomplish what I have asked this time, **Do Not Bother To Return**. You are dismissed."

Drate storms out of the room, tumbling the little rodent demons like dried leaves as he passes them on his way out. His mouth moves, but no words come out. Everyone knows better than to even look at Drate when he is like this. Almost everything makes him mad, but the thing that starts flames hurling from his nostrils faster than anything else, is when he is humiliated. Humble is not a word Drate is familiar with. Humility is a sign of weakness in his opinion. To be less than equal to anyone is unheard of. In

Warning. This Is A Test. This Is Only A Test.

most cases, he feels himself superior to everyone. As he disappears into the distance, you can hear him roaring and cursing. **"This - is - not - a - job - for - a - future - lord**."

The Care Flight Helicopter, crew, and patient, arrive at the hospital in record time. Gunther is leading the way, seeing to it that there aren't any delays. Doctor Jeffreys, the doctor on staff for the evening, and the emergency room technicians are ready and waiting for the patient to arrive. They've communicated with the Emergency Medical Technicians as they transported the patient into town. The x-ray and operating rooms have been prepped by the nurses and their staff. They are ready to go. The gurney is rolled into the emergency room about the same time Victoria Arrington arrives at the front desk of the hospital asking about her husband.

Kreig spots Gunther and nods.

You can hear the doctor and the E. M. T's discussing the latest condition as the doors to the emergency room swing open and shut. They begin to work trying to save the life of this very critically injured, thirty-two year old man. Doctor Jeffreys and a sea of nurses surround the table. All you see are caps and gowns moving around the table, reaching, passing instruments, and pointing. The door opens again. They're on the way to the x-ray room.

Around the first corner, Victoria meets the gurney head on. She stops in her tracks, and her hand immediately covers her mouth as she gasps. Her heart seems to stop, and she can't move, as the gurney continues on around her.

In passing, Gunther alerts Kreig of the onslot of opposition. "My Brother, the forces are gathering in huge masses." He nods, and continues to follow the gurney.

"We are prepared to do battle." Kreig loudly announces.

Nurse Esther Walsh, a small brunette following the gurney, stops to see if she can help this bewildered looking, lady. Recognizing her as an old school mate, she asks, "Victoria, Victoria Miller? Aren't you a Miller?"

Victoria keeps her eyes on the gurney, never hearing anyone speaking to her.

"It's Esther. What in the world are you doing up here?" She has no idea the latest emergency case is Victoria's husband. The two women lost contact with each other when Esther went away to nursing school.

Victoria is still oblivious to everything around her; she seems to be staring off into space, but she is very focused, her eyes are following the man being taken down the hall.

Esther calls her name again, then touches her on the arm.

The spirit Confusion, is thronging her mind. This is all out war, and the enemy is having the time of their life.

Victoria looks at her with confusion and total disbelief. "Is that my husband that just went by on

Warning. This Is A Test. This Is Only A Test.

that table? Where are they taking him? What happened?" Her questions are coming too fast and too numerous to be answered.

Esther takes her by the arm and leads her to the waiting room. She appears to be in shock. "Calm down now. He's just arriving and we don't know much about his condition just yet. I'll see what I can find out for you, but all I know so far is that he's had an accident on his job; something fell on him." Esther should have been a doctor; she has a natural uplifting bedside manner.

"When can I see him? I need to see him." She's wringing her hands out of nervousness. If she could just see him or touch him!

"What is your husbands name?" Esther tries to get her focus onto something else.

"Mitch, his name is Mitch." She says his name like it was the last time she'd ever hear it.

"Is there anyone I can call to come and sit with you? It may be a while before we know anything about Mitch." She's more aware of the seriousness of Mitch's condition than she's letting on. She'd been in the room when the vitals were first being reported.

Victoria's mind is going back to this morning. How glad she is at this moment that she had taken the time to pray. Realizing that she'd been asked a question, she responds, sounding a bit unsure of her answer. "Uh,...yes,... I need to call my mother. She has my children, and I need to call our Pastor."

Esther directs her to the nurses station to make the calls. "I'll see what I can find out for you."

Still smoldering from the scorching he'd received earlier and still muttering to himself, Drate is going to get this thing over with, and show those brainless, wanna be demons, who is on the job! As he nears the hospital he tries to convince himself that this is going to be a snap. "This won't take but just a minute and I'll be gone." He tells himself.

Across the horizon, to the east, a shimmer of light catches his eye. "I don't have time to play right now, my little winged do-gooders. I have business to attend to and you will just have to wait." His pride has been wounded, his ability to handle a simple job has been called to question, and on top of all that, he's having to deal with Gunther. He's not going to be able to take much more. Like a loose keg of nitroglycerin, he could blow up at any time.

Unfortunately, he isn't being given a choice. The game is planned, and he has already been chosen as one of the key players. His feeling of superiority is about to become his downfall.

With the phone to her ear, Victoria hears her mother's voice on the other end. "Hello."

"Mom, I'm at the hospital. Mitch has had a very serious accident. I don't have much more to tell you now, but I'll let you know later how things are going." She's rambling on, trying hard not to break into tears.

Warning. This Is A Test. This Is Only A Test.

"Oh Darlin', I'm so sorry." Ruth can tell Victoria's under a tremendous load. "Hun, do you need me to come down? Is there something I can do?"

Discouragement and Fear, are back to take another shot at breaking down the Arrington lady.

Kreig stands his post.

"No Mom, I'm gonna be fine. I'm gonna call Reverend McAllister. They'll come." Her voice is fading in and out as her mind wanders.

"What are you going to do, a widow at such a young age?" Fear taunts.

Victoria shakes her head, trying to shake free from the voices in her mind.

"Well now, if you can't get the McAllisters, call me back, and I'll be there as soon as I can get there." Ruth loves her daughter and is always willing to be there for her, but knows she needs her to watch the children right now.

"You need to go pick up the children's overnight bags with a few changes of clothes, and wait to hear from me." The stress is easily detected in her voice.

Discouragement chimes in, "You won't be here very long, he's not going to live much longer."

Fighting back the devils of hell, she adds, "Oh, and Mom, call everyone to pray, this could be serious." Tears run down her petite face. She can't hold the tears back any longer. Saying the words makes it sound so definite.

"Darlin', don't you worry any at all about these children. They'll be just fine. Now you take care of yourself and be there for Mitch. I know I don't have to worry about you. You have always been so strong. I love you." In her absence she's trying to plant hope in her heart.

"Thanks, Mom. I knew I could count on you." It's times like this that makes her want to be just like her mother.

"Is there any news at all? Do you know how the accident happened?" Ruth tries to shift the subject away from herself, and back to Mitch.

"Not yet. They've just taken him down to X-ray. I've not been able to talk to anyone that has any information yet." She says through her tears.

Discouragement and Fear continue to bombard her mind with a blast of negative thoughts.

"Well, keep us up on his condition. Don't worry about us."

"I will Mom. Bye, and thanks again." With the receiver in her hand, she stands motionless, fighting back the river of tears she can feel welling up from deep within her soul.

As the mid-day sky becomes more gray-green, and the air becomes a bit more chilled, the forecaster is predicting rain, possible freezing rain, and maybe some early morning snow. This is typical of Texas weather, the days can be so warm that you work up a sweat, and in the evening you may need a fire in the fireplace. It is one of the things Texans love about their home. That and the fact that they don't have to deal with snow plows and being snowed in for days. Variety is their spice of life, that, and of course jalapeno peppers.

Warning. This Is A Test. This Is Only A Test.

The next phone call goes to the Pastor's home. They are just sitting down to their late afternoon meal as the call comes in. The McAllisters have learned to eat when they are ready. It never fails if they wait until meal time to eat, they are going to most likely do without. In-between charity functions, funerals, weddings, hospital visits, conference time, and their own personal lives, they are more than busy. Especially these last few months. It seems like everyone is in need of prayer and they are certainly willing to do whatever it takes to be there for the Church family and the community.

Across town the McAllister's phone rings. Pastor McAllister folds his napkin and places it in his chair as he stands to take the call. "Hello."

"Pastor, this is Victoria Arrington. I'm at the hospital." Her voice is noticeably troubled. "I don't know what's happened, yet. I just arrived myself."

"Slow down now. Everything's gonna be okay." He motions to his wife to stay seated.

"They've brought Mitch in. He's had an accident and we need you and the church to pray." She's pacing the floor as she tries to explain and make some sense out of the little bit of information she has.

"We will notify the prayer hot line and get a prayer chain started right now. My wife and I will be there as soon as we can. Are you at County Memorial?"

"Yes, County Memorial." She tries so hard to swallow, but the lump in her throat seems to be cutting off her air.

"We're on our way." He says.

"Thank you. I appreciate it." Victoria returns to the emergency room waiting area, and in no time at all, the gurney that is carrying her husband rolls by on it's way back to the emergency room once again. She stands to catch a glimpse and sees that he's bruised, swollen, and bloody. The only way she can really tell it is Mitch is the uniform.

Esther comes up from behind her, "Victoria, I have some news for you." She takes her to the nearest chair. "The machinery that fell on your husband has done a lot of damage. Now, the doctor is working to see what would be the best procedure. He'll be out with you in a few minutes. Doctor Jeffreys is a wonderful doctor." She sees hurting people every day, and still seeing someone struggle with bad news touches her soft heart.

The room, full of demons, imps, and devas, are shouting, and dancing.

Kreig moves in a little closer to Victoria and dares anyone to even look her way. With his sword in his hand, and a look of mischief on his face, he convinces the demons to back up just a bit. He can't keep her from being tested, but he can give her periods of rest.

Victoria turns her head away to look out the window, and tries to hold herself together. The rain begins to fall like it is being poured from a bucket. That is exactly how she feels. Like she's been poured out, and is empty. "What exactly is wrong?" her shaky voice asks.

Warning. This Is A Test. This Is Only A Test.

"They've taken X-rays. There appears to be several broken bones and he has a collapsed lung. The blow to the head may have caused some unknown damage and, for now, that's all we know. We'll know more when the other X-rays are read. Wait for the doctor, and he will have a full report."

"Thank you so much. I appreciate all you've done." Victoria manages a little smile, despite the fact that the news she's just received feels like a ton of bricks piled on her chest.

"You're most welcome. It is my pleasure." Esther wishes there was more she could say or do. "Did you make your calls? Is someone coming to be with you?" She knows this has been hard on her, and having someone close, a familiar shoulder to cry on, is always good.

"Yes, I have people coming. Thank you." She wipes the stream of tears from her anxious face, and tries to stay in control.

"Well, if there's anything else I can do for you just let me know." Duty calls, but she is going to keep a close watch on Victoria until someone comes to be with her.

In the silence, the fear almost seems audible. Every crack and crevice of the hospital walls are glowing from the sulfur colored eyes of demons, imps, and evil spirits. What a perfect place to be stationed. There are more hearts and minds in this one place in a day to assault than any other place in town. The fact that they are under duress when they come in here, makes it even easier to infiltrate their minds, and cause added stress. An unguarded mind is truly the devils playground.

    Kreig senses Victoria needs another break from the constant tormenting. Drawing in all the air his lungs can hold, he lets out a war cry, and demons scatter like their tails are on fire. He strokes her mind with peace and rest. The demons will be back, and in stronger force.

Luke 11:24-26

24 When the unclean spirit is gone out of a man, he walketh through dry places, seeking rest; and finding none, he saith, I will return unto my house whence I came out.

25 And when he cometh, he findeth it swept and garnished.

26 Then goeth he, and taketh to him seven other spirits more wicked than himself; and they enter in, and dwell there: and the last state of that man is worse than the first.

(KJV)

Warning. This Is A Test. This Is Only A Test.

Reinforcements

7

The Pastor and his wife arrive just in time to help Victoria hold up under the strain of not knowing exactly what's going on. "Oh, Reverend and Mrs. McAllister, I'm so glad you're here." She allows herself to break down into tears.

Valek and The Bishop have also arrived. They are the constant and loyal angelic companions of the McAllisters.

Six weeks ago, when the McAllisters and their congregation issued a challenge to the prince of darkness seated in their town, Valek, and The Bishop, entered into continual warfare with the enemy. Tinga didn't take the initial challenge too seriously. It was when the church actually got down to business, followed through with fervent prayer, and fasting, with a goal in mind, perfecting unity among themselves, and devoting their all to the cause, that the message was made clear. Then and only then was the attention of Tinga gained.

Standing guard at the waiting room door is Kreig, Victoria's guardian angel. "Greetings my brothers."

The Bishop, and Valek greet Kreig.

Mrs. McAllister sits down beside Victoria to be a comfort. That is all that is necessary from Mrs. McAllister. Just having her there was what Victoria needs.

The door to the waiting room opens and the doctor walks in asking for, " Mrs. Arrington."

"I'm Victoria Arrington." She says, as she jumps to her feet. "How is my husband? When can I see him?" She was an erupting volcano of questions.

"I'm Doctor Jeffreys, and I'll be the doctor in charge of your husband's care. First, I'd like for you to sit down and try to relax. How are you holding up?" He smiles his award winning smile. "Would you like for me to prescribe something to calm your nerves?" He has no doubt she's to the point of exploding from the pressure she's under.

"Oh no, I'm fine. How is my husband ?" She has one thing on her mind, and it's not her condition.

"Well, it's complicated at this point. We are still waiting for x-rays to tell us the whole story, but from what I can see, it appears to be serious. You have some decisions to make and they need to be made now. I'm sorry. I don't mean to seem so crass, but time is not something we have a lot of." It's an awesome responsibility, having a life in your hands and being asked to make zero mistakes. Fortunately for Doctor Jeffreys, God is having His way in this entire situation.

Warning. This Is A Test. This Is Only A Test.

Overhead, the deflated ego of Drate begins to regain it's normal, or in his case abnormal, size. He's convinced himself, once again, that soon he'll be in control of the largest area in the state, and then **no** one will tell him what to do! He spirals through the hospital roof, down to the emergency room waiting area, where Victoria and the McAllisters are waiting. "Oh, the poor lady must be getting the bad news." He says sarcastically as he saunters into the waiting room. He wants to get an up close look at the doctor and Mrs. Arrington. He wants to hear first hand all the gory details about how poor Mitch Arrington has only minutes to live, or even better, how he's no longer in the land of the living.

Pastor and Mrs. McAllister feel the chilling presence of the demon as he slithers into the room. Softly speaking a prayer, they feel the presence of the Lord fill the room. Kreig, Valek, and The Bishop, are on top of the situation. Valek and The Bishop each grab an arm, and quickly escort Drate out of the hospital kicking and screaming.

The weather outside is getting colder by the minute, and the wet roads are beginning to ice over. This is going to be a rough night all the way around.

Victoria's sister, Cricket, rushes to her side, escorted by Strom, a valiant warrior. "I'm sorry it's taken me so long to get here. Mom left a message on my machine." She exhales, and takes a deep breath. Giving Victoria a hug, she says, "I'm sorry, I've interrupted you." She settles back and listens to the doctor explain Mitch's condition.

Strom joins the other angelic host.

Continuing, the doctor says, "Mrs. Arrington, I don't want to frighten you, but your husband's condition is very critical, and I need your permission to do surgery."

She hadn't expected this kind of news. "Surgery? Oh God!" She cries out for inner strength.

Kreig is right there to comfort her in his special way with the Words from the Lord.

Cricket squeezes one hand, and Mrs. McAllister the other, trying to comfort her.

"The machine that fell on your husband has broken several bones, collapsed a lung, and there is internal bleeding inside his skull. I'll know more about his condition when I get in there." He's trying his best to be brief, yet open with her.

"When do you need to have my answer?" Looking around the room, she is hoping someone will offer the answer to this million dollar question.

"The sooner the better." He's aware of the seriousness of Mitch's condition and knows time is not something he has a lot of.

" May I see him now?" She needs to see him for herself.

"Of course, but only for a minute." The young doctor escorts her to the room where her husband lays silent like a corpse.

Drate tries to tag along. The sight of blood and the feeling of pain are one of his joys. Kreig, Valek, Strom, and The Bishop, are there to convince him to stay out.

Drate's temper is flaring, this is not the song and dance he wants to hear, and he is getting tired of

Warning. This Is A Test. This Is Only A Test.

these bullies messing up his plans. He's going to plan B, the fear tactic. It works like a charm. "If she doesn't sign, Mitch won't live and I'll be done with this cheesy job. Just look at him. There's no way he'll be here after an hour or two. With him dead, I'll be praised, and that's as it should be." There was only one thing Drate hadn't considered, Gunther. The massive, heavenly warrior, is at his post. He is now blocked on all sides.

Cricket and the McAllisters make their way to the coffee machine.

"I'm so glad you came. The roads outside are really icing over fast." Cricket says offering Mrs. McAllister a cup of hot coffee. "She needs someone here with her."

"We arrived before the roads started icing over." Mrs. McAllister says as she takes the hot coffee.

As Victoria opens the door to the emergency room, she stops and whispers a prayer for strength and wisdom. The prayer is heard, and orders are sent to Kreig to stand close to her this night and see that she has the added strength she needs. Coming closer to the gurney, she sees that Mitch has his eyes open, and he ever so slowly turns to look at her.

"Mitch." her voice cracks. "Mitch, it's Victoria." She's relieved to see him, but it's taking everything within her not to break down.

The tubes and I. V. bags hanging everywhere make him look even worse. He nods an affirmative nod, and turns his palm up to take her hand. She responds by taking his hand in both of her feminine hands. It is like an exchange of silent communication. No words are spoken, but the message is received on both ends. Everything will be okay.

In the next room, Drate tries to convince the warriors to let him finish the job. "Oh, please, people, let's face the facts that this is the end. I want to be on my way. Give it up." As he leans forward to take a step closer, his feet seem to be hanging in mid-air. "**What's going on here?**" he whines.

"Well, Drate, I knew you weren't gonna stick to the original plans. You'll never change. I made it my business to keep an eye on you." With Gunther's massive hands on Drate's shoulders, he lifts Drate off the floor.

Drate fights desperately to get loose. "**Put me down!**" He screams.

Trying his best to be very precise, Gunther chooses his words carefully. "The **only** thing that you have permission to do **has - already - been - done**. I'd suggest you go back where you came from and leave the rest to us." Gunther means what he says, as he drops the bag of bad news to the floor.

It doesn't take Drate long to disappear, but he isn't going too far. Not just yet.

In the emergency room, Victoria's visit is cut short. "Mrs. Arrington, you'll have to wait outside." Doctor Jeffreys says, as he makes his way back into the room. Esther leads her to the door.

"I need your decision, Mrs. Arrington. Time is critical to your husband's condition." He warns, as she exits the room.

Warning. This Is A Test. This Is Only A Test.

She slowly makes her way back to the emergency room waiting area. Her mind is racing. "What to do God? What to do?" She repeats over and over.

"Victoria, how is he?" Cricket helps her sister to a chair. It's obvious, by the washed out look on her face, that she is carrying a heavy load. "Oh, Mitch's boss is here."

She'd not even noticed. "Oh, Mr. Henderson." She acknowledges he is there with her mouth, but her brain can't register all that's going on. The willingness to be polite and social is there, but the mind is not able.

"Mrs. Arrington, I'm so sorry about the accident. I got here as soon as I could, but the roads are getting bad out." It is Vernon, the County Road Commissioner. With hat in hand he tries to convey how he's feeling, but it's just not easy. Mitch has been in his employment for twelve years, and in that time they've grown close.

"Oh, Mr. Henderson, thank you for coming. Mitch would be glad to know you are here." She can see the worry on his face, and appreciates his concern.

"How is he?" Vernon asked with a look of anxiety on his face. He's expecting to hear bad news. He'd talked to Corky on his cell phone on the way over and had some idea of the seriousness of Mitch's injuries.

"They say his right lung has collapsed, there are broken bones, and some damage to his head. That's all I know right now. They need me to sign release forms to do surgery." She's still not comfortable about making a decision.

"If there's anything I can do just let me know. We are all so sorry." He continues to apologize as though it were somehow his fault.

"Thank you. All we need right now is prayer, and God will help Mitch come out of this okay." She is trying to keep her thoughts and energy focused on the only hope they have, Jesus.

"We'll certainly be doing that."

Drate is not a happy camper. He was booted out of the meeting by that power crazed Tinga, and later ordered around like he was an upstart by that nobody, Gunther. The others are laughing at him like he was some rookie. He is just having a bad hair day. Come to think of it, Drate is always having a bad hair day. Pondering his next move, he is distracted by a haunting sound coming from out of the east. As he turns to see what it could be, he spots Grice. He is singing the new rap song he's made up about himself.

"I'm bad, so bad , the meanest demon , who is so rad. You mess with me, I'll beat you down. I'm bad, so bad."

The noise is unbearable. "What are you doing here, Grice?" Drate growls. "Lost your way to the game room again?" He sneers.

Grice is beaming with delight. "Nope, I've been sent with orders, orders to help you." Tinga has sent him to again, help Drate. They both know this won't set well; he thinks of himself as independent, and self sufficient.

Warning. This Is A Test. This Is Only A Test.

"**Help me? Ha? By - whose - orders?**" Drate is frothing at the mouth. First, it is Gunther ordering him around, then Tinga, now, some runt of a nobody!

With his arms crossed behind his back, Grice just smiles his mischievous smile, and enjoys the frustrated look on Drate's face. He knows after Drate finishes with his ranting and raving and he hears Tinga's orders, there will be nothing else he can say about the matter.

"**I need your help like I need that know it all, Gunther, messing up things. Now be gone or I'll slice you into little pieces**." Drate is about ready to come apart at the seams.

Feeling a bit more feisty than usual, Grice smirks and gives a cocky response. "Sorry, no can do. Tinga said to stick with you like glue, and he also said if you give me any lip, he'll take care of you himself."

Drate clinches his teeth and gives a low guttural growl. "Fine - then, fine." He spins away from Grice. "Just stay out of my way and maybe you'll learn something about being a great warrior. Not that you'll ever be one." Drate has a unique way of turning everything around, in his mind, to make it look like he's still in control.

Gunther, Kreig, Strom, Valek, and The Bishop, get together to discuss the battle strategy.

"What is your plan, friend? How do you intend on handling this Drate character?" asks The Bishop.

"I've given him the last chance to leave by his own power." Gunther states emphatically. "I guess this calls for more drastic measures. But first, I'd like to teach him a lesson."

"Can we be of any help?" Valek perks up, hoping to be included in the plans. Teaching these kind of lessons is what Valek lives for.

"I believe you just might be able to help me. Are you game for a little cat and mouse?" Gunther gets a slight curl in the right corner of his mouth and raises his eyebrows up just a bit.

Everyone smiles and nods. This is going to be interesting.

Poor Grice. He's gonna regret not taking Drate's advice and going anywhere except here. The games are about to begin, and those who are not on the Lord's side are about to be personally introduced to the omnipotent power, of the Almighty, via His host of angelic warriors.

In the emergency room waiting area, Mr. Henderson once again offers his apologies and excuses himself.

Since Victoria is still not fully in tune with all that's going on, Cricket replies for her. "She has so much on her mind. I apologize." Walking with him down the hall, "I know they both appreciate you coming by. She's still in shock over the whole thing."

"Oh, I understand completely. Please tell her if there's anything I can do, all she needs to do is call." He places his big black Stetson firmly on his head, turns up the wool collar on his overcoat, and darts out into the blowing snow.

"I will, and thanks again for coming." She says hurrying back into the building, away from the sharp,

Warning. This Is A Test. This Is Only A Test.

bone chilling wind, that's howling through the open doors.

Victoria and the McAllisters have resumed their conversation, and the talk turns to the surgery.

"I know he needs the surgery, but I'm sort of afraid...... I know in my heart God can, but...... in my mind I wonder if He will!" Letting go of what seems right, and taking a chance on what she knows to be right, is somehow frightening.

Drate hears the word afraid and jumps on it like a kite taken by a strong March wind. But his very next thought is interrupted by the towering shadows of Gunther, Kreig, Strom, Valek, and the awesomely tall Bishop. As he turns to see what could be causing this dark cloud hovering around him, it disappears as mysteriously, and as fast, as it came.

Grice is staying out of sight just like he was told. From his hiding place he has a perfect view of Drate and the angelic fighting five. He is having the time of his life.

"Let's pray. I know God wants you to feel peace about your decision, He's just the one to give you the peace you need and help you to do the right thing." The Reverend McAllister reaches to his wife and Victoria.

Cricket makes her way back into the room, and joins the threesome.

On hearing these words, Drate spins back around. Back to the matter at hand. "**Why can't these people leave well enough alone?**" He roars.

Out of the corner of his fiery red eyes, he sees something rushing toward him. He jumps out of the way. When he stands to his feet, there's nothing there. "All right Grice, that's about enough of this horse play. Who do you think you're dealing with here?" Every hair on his body is bristled, his anger has just peeked to a new, all time high. Pressures are mounting and he's about to lose control.

Grice gives no answer, but he laughs even louder, hoping not to be heard. He covers his mouth with his furry little paw.

The prayers are being prayed and they are getting on the last frayed nerve Drate has left. "I'll show these pests who's running this show." His nostrils flare, his face turns an even deeper shade of red, and his back arches like the hump on a brahma bull. As he lunges toward the prayer group, the three warriors step out in his path. Like a crazed, charging bull, he smashes into the angelic brick wall, and knocks himself out cold.

Doctor Jeffreys enters the room just as the prayer closes. "Mrs. Arrington, I really don't mean to rush you, but --- "

Victoria interrupts his sentence. "Yes, Doctor, do whatever you have to do. I know God's hand is on Mitch and he'll guide your hands as well. I'll sign whatever you need signed."

Drate is still lying in a heap on the floor. No longer does he convey the image of strength, and wild brute force. You can even say he has a look of serenity to him, but of course no one would ever think of saying that to Drate!

Warning. This Is A Test. This Is Only A Test.

Gunther spots a little creature hiding in the shadows. "Little demon, I'm giving you one second to disappear. If I look up again and see your beady little eyes glowing, you're gonna be reduced to a spot on the floor. Now - **scat**!" Clapping his hands together, making a loud popping noise, he turns and smiles at his fellow warriors.

Grice doesn't waste any time. Like a bullet shot out of a high powered rifle, he's out of sight before you can blink.

Gunther, Kreig, Strom, Valek, and The Bishop, have a good laugh as Grice leaves only a puff of smoke where he had once crouched.

**Leviticus 26:8 And five of you shall chase an hundred, and an hundred of you shall put ten thousand to flight: and your enemies shall fall before you by the sword.
(KJV)**

Warning. This Is A Test. This Is Only A Test.

Mountains Of Steel

8

Back at the hive, Tinga and his swarm of dedicated followers wait for word of a great victory from Drate. A thunderous noise is heard, followed by the stump, Grice, as he comes tumbling in completely out of breath and tired to the bone. He rolls into his little corner and collapses. When he finally regains his breath, he begins to snicker to himself. Soon a crowd has gathered. It isn't very often that anyone is this happy around here, about anything!

"What's his problem?" One of the scoundrels asks.

"His small mind must have finally burnt out on him!" Another remarks sarcastically.

"No, no, you gotta hear this." Grice gasps for another breath of air. "I've just left Drate!" He's laughing so hard he has to pause to catch his breath. The mention of Drate really gets everyone's attention. Not too many are very fond of Drate, mostly because of his arrogant attitude. "There we were, tending to the business at hand, and out of nowhere, four of the biggest mountains of steel stepped out in front of Drate. He was like a runaway locomotive, charging at a group of praying mortals."

"Well, what happened? Tell us what happened." The growing crowd cheers for more information.

"Well, now he's laid out cold as a wedge." Grice is beaming with sheer satisfaction. He's lived to see the day when Drate was given some of his own medicine.

"Who was it?" several voices chime in at one time. The unruly crowd continues to get larger.

Grice is loving the attention this is getting him. No one ever pays him the slightest bit of attention. "Okay, okay, calm down and I'll tell you every little detail." With his arms raised above his pointed head, to exaggerate his point, he begins naming the warriors off one by one. "Gunther, the warrior that is responsible for our beloved Tinga having only one hand and also the scar that Drate is so defensive of, he was there." He says softly, not wanting to be overheard by Tinga.

"Gunther? I thought he was in India guarding some missionary!" The demon Gossip, replies in awe.

Grice continues to list the elite group. "The other was Kreig, the mighty German whose name means, '**Current of Electricity**'. Strom, he was one of the mighty warriors used to hold back the Red Sea." A look of joy comes over his face, he's having a flash back. "I'll never forget that day. We didn't get rid of those Israelites, but it was almost as much fun

Warning. This Is A Test. This Is Only A Test.

seeing all those soldiers and horses drowning!" Everyone is spell bound, they can't believe what they are hearing. "Oh yea, Valek, he was assigned to Job's side. We all know how that turned out! Last, but not least, was The Bishop."

The gearing crowd gasps, "The Bishop?"

"Yep, the ten and a half foot tall giant killer, you all remember he's the force that was used to hurl the stone at Goliath of Gath, when David went to battle for his people." Grice is using facial expressions, hand gestures, and noises, to exaggerate his point. Although he's not exaggerating anything he's said about the angelic host. They are all he says and more.

"These guys sound a little bit out of Drate's league." The strong dislike they feel for Drate drives them to secretly cheer for the Host of Heaven. Only this once of course.

Grice continues to tell of the mighty warrior's victories. "These are also the warriors that were there when the walls of Jerico came tumbling down. It was another day of victory for the Israelites. The host stood in the center of the city and when the trump sounded they all four rushed at their appointed wall and it came down like sand being washed away by a mammoth wave." Grice envies the power and accomplishments of these great victors.

"What about Drate? What did these fellows do to Drate?" All ears are tuned to hear the fate that was dealt to Drate.

Happy to tell, he continues, "The high and mighty Drate just laid there like a pile of dirty laundry on the floor after he ran into the wall of steel." Everyone gets a good laugh. Grice gladly repeats the story as it circulates in every corner of the camp.

P icking himself up off the floor, Drate is slowly coming around. The warriors have long since left to check on the progress of Mitch Arrington and to make sure Mrs. Arrington isn't bothered by **anyone**.

Victoria's on the phone letting her Mother know the updated news and telling the children goodnight.

Mrs. Miller answers the phone sounding anxious. She's hoping to hear good news about Mitch. "Hello."

"Mom, how's everything going?" Exhausted from all that she's been through, she takes this opportunity to sit down and close her eyes.

"Calls have been coming in all evening, Victoria, asking about Mitch. I have nothing to tell them, but that he is in God's hands."

"Well, Mom, they're getting him ready for surgery right now. I'll call you when we have news." She's sounds tired, frustrated, and ready for this to all be over. "Are the children around? I want to tell them goodnight."

"Certainly. They're standing right here." She hands the phone to Nicole.

Warning. This Is A Test. This Is Only A Test.

"Hello, Mommy." She's excited to hear her mother's voice.

"Hi, Baby. Are you taking good care of everything for me?"

"We made chocolate chip cookies and Pa let us go fishing." Her little voice was filled with joy.

"That's great, I just called to say goodnight, and to tell you that I love you."

"Chase ate four cookies, and drank two whole glasses of milk."

"Well, is Chase there? Can I talk to him now?"

"Okay, but can I tell you one more thing?" This sounds important.

"Mommy?" She tries to be so big.

"Yes, Nicole."

"I - love - you."

"I love you too, baby, and I'll see you soon. Now put Chase on the phone."

"Hi, Mommy. Did Nicole tell you I caught a big bass?" Chase sounds like he's having a great time.

"Really, well good for you. Now listen, I'm gonna be here at the hospital all night and I need you to help take care of things. Can you do that for me?"

"Yes Ma'am, but Mom?"

"Yes, Son."

"Is it okay if we sleep in the tent tonight? Pa says he wants to." He's all boy.

"Sure, if Pa wants to, we wouldn't want to let him down." She's happy that her children like to be at her folks' place. She knows she doesn't have to worry about them.

"Thanks, Mom, I gotta go now. Pa says I can help hammer the tent." He's anxious to get started on this wild excursion. He hands the phone back to Gran and he's off to the back yard.

"Well, as you heard they're doing okay. Now don't you worry about us. We're all fine." Ruby reassures.

"I know Mom. Thanks for everything. I'm gonna go now. Tell Dad I said to not let Chase talk him into anything too wild." She knows how big of a push over her Dad is when it come to Nicole and Chase. "I'll call you tomorrow."

"Okay, I'll talk to you tomorrow."

As Victoria puts the phone down, a chill goes up her spine. In the spirit world a hair raising roar is heard. Gunther and his friends are more than ready. Like an out of control freight train, Drate comes barreling down the corridors of the hospital determined to put an end to this game and finish Mitch Arrington for good. Through clinched teeth, he screams a word for every step he pounds out with his huge clawed feet. **"These - are - my - rules - we - are - playing - by, - choir - boys, - and - I - intend - on - taking - this - mortal - out! My - promotion - is - in - the - bag! Now - move - it - or - lose - it!"** Angry would not come close to describing his demeanor. Crazed is more of an appropriate description.

Gunther shrugs his massive shoulders and smiles a mischievous smile. " You heard what he said, fellow warriors! I gladly except his challenge. In fact, I think it's the best idea he's ever had."

Warning. This Is A Test. This Is Only A Test.

Kreig is more than ready to do battle, "This should be fun, comrades! I except."

The Bishop, Strom and Valek all agree this is what they've all been waiting for, an opportunity to give Drate what he deserves. "The vote is unanimous my brothers."

They all stand shoulder to shoulder making it impossible for anything to pass, but Drate is too far gone. His adrenaline is past the boiling point, and it is do or die for him. He'd been shamed by Tinga in front of an underling, made to fill inadequate to handle this job, assaulted by Gunther and his friends, bombarded with prayer, and now this! This game has ceased to be fun and he's ready to put an end to the angelic beings who are causing him so much trouble.

Victoria feels that urging that she'd felt earlier that day. The drowsiness that was creeping up on her left immediately. She finds herself praying and asking God for power to defeat the enemy. Unaware of the danger that she and Mitch are in, she gets down to business and power is given.

Drate hits the wall of heavenly metal with such force, on impact he causes a loud explosive noise, a puff of smoke, and he is history.

Grice and his fellow nasties' laughter, is silenced by the chilling vibes that echo through the atmosphere.

"Trouper, Trouper, report to me at once!" screams Tinga.

Trouper is at the side of his master and lord in a flash. He knows the tone of his master's voice means someone is gonna have problems, and he doesn't want it to be him. "Yes, your mighty one! Your loyal and obedient servant is here. What may I do for you?"

"**I feel trouble in my bones. Something has just happened to alter my plans. Who has dared disobey me?**" His voice carries through the halls of their hideout and into the night, having the effect of a moderate sized typhoon. The reverberations tumble imps as they go about doing their chores, Tinga letting everyone within a fifty mile radius know, he is upset **again**!"

"Oh, no one, I assure you, no one would dare disobey you, my lord." The scrawny imp grovels.

"Oh, pipe down you brainless footstool, and call a meeting. I want all of my captains here within the hour. Send runners and leave someone to guard their post," Tinga demands, slamming his fist down on the arm of his majestic throne. Continuing to growl, grumble and talk to himself as he paces back and forth, like a caged tiger, his arms are flailing around missing the little imp attending him by only a fraction of an inch each time he swings. "Out of my way!" He screams as he shoves the imp in the direction of the door. "I need my space, time to think. I do not want to be bothered until all of my captains are here. Now out of my sight!"

Never has anyone seen Tinga so outraged.

Warning. This Is A Test. This Is Only A Test.

Gunther and the others are ready. They are aware of the fact that getting rid of Drate is only going to be the beginning. If the Arringtons are truly a threat to the local covenant of darkness, they'll not give up so easily.

Meanwhile, surgery is about to begin on Mitch. The bleeding in his head is becoming more critical, and the lung that has collapsed will be a big threat to him the longer they wait.

The McAllisters, Cricket, and Victoria find a place in the hospital's Chapel to pray.

Prayer is going up all over the world. The International Network Of Prayer has sent out a call for prayer warriors everywhere to pray for Mitch Arrington. The will of God will be done this day, despite the horrendous efforts of Tinga and his cohorts. The Church knows that the enemy doesn't give up easy and they are here until a victory report comes in.

Gunther and friends are pleased. "It would be nice if all our jobs were this easy, but for some reason the mortals can't seem to understand the effect their prayer has on them personally, and the world around them in general. The power we have can only be obtained from their prayers."

The conclave is in session and heads will roll if this problem isn't resolved, to the letter, in a very short time. Tinga is frothing at the mouth with anger, and the air is clouded with the fumes from his heated words. Reports come in of the defeat and termination of Drate. Humiliated and disgusted, Tinga has to reassign the effort to another. Tinga first has to ask himself, "which bumbling idiot, which brainless moron, will I send to do this simple task?"

Numbers 22:22 And the angel of the LORD stood in the way for an adversary against him.

Psalms 34:7 The angel of the LORD encampeth round about them that fear him, and delivereth them. **(KJV)**

Warning. This Is A Test. This Is Only A Test.

The Take Over

9

From the back of the dark, crowded room, an unfamiliar voice emphatically states. "**I am here to rid your region of this plague of Christians.**" The force behind the words send chills over the leathery hides of the assembly. Every eye strains to focus on the dark corner. The very hair on their leathery bodies raise to attention, every fiber of their being is focusing on the one unidentified, mysterious voice. Who could this be with such boldness, to come in on a meeting, and take the floor from Tinga without first being granted permission? The captains are all waiting for Tinga's response and Tinga is simply glad he isn't here alone. How did this intruder gain entrance into Tinga's private chambers? There was nothing but silence, and a dreadful cold chill in the air, as those gathered stood in fear waiting for the trespasser to reveal himself.

Finally, from the veil of the dark corner, the enormous mass of muscle and brawn steps out and the flickering candlelight hits his princely, noble profile. What a surprise! This can't be, this just can't be. Shock and disbelief has overwhelmed everyone in the room. No one can believe that someone so powerful and influential would belittle himself to enter this dirty little hideaway. Why had he personally come and not sent a messenger? But here he stands, as big as life itself. The infamous Governor Sterben. Like a bronze statue, he has a jaw of steel, and his eyes are a penetrating light, seemingly scorching your inner being as he peers through you. His stance is that of royalty. His cloak is what appears to be spun gold. Everything about his demeanor attests to his regal position. As he steps out into the room, everyone, including Tinga, falls to the floor, partly out of obeisance but mainly out of fear. This is no time to squabble over position or dispute ethics pertaining to rank. The Prince of darkness has personally sent his Governor of Militant Forces to take charge and mop this thing up before it gets out of hand. It is obviously a bigger deal than anyone here has thought.

Gunther and his fellow warriors are feeling the effect the flood of prayers are having on them. Their minds are growing more astute, muscles are hardening, and their bodies seem stronger than they ever remembered them being before. The question

Warning. This Is A Test. This Is Only A Test.

arose as to why this one man was so important. Why was so much fuss being made for a mere mortal? They'd battled demonic forces, won wars, and fought the enemy on several occasions before. But this is different. Why so many of us? They know in their hearts more hostile forces are to come, but why so many? Maybe there is more to this than meets the eye. No matter. The task is at hand. They've been allotted the honor of fighting this fight, and fight they will. To the death, of the enemy that is!

"Arise, little ones. Victory is yours this day. Let us make preparations to end this game we are playing with the heavenly creatures and be done with it." Governor Sterben boasts, as he makes his way to the speaking podium at the opposite end of the room.

With each step the Governor so carefully takes crossing the meeting hall, he painstakingly makes eye contact with the demons standing about the room. When the breeze caused by his flowing cape blows across their faces and into their nostrils, it has the sedating effect of a well cast spell. His mere presence has a calming effect on the congregation. Their gaping mouths are transformed into silly school girl grins. The fear they had been feeling is now melted into total and absolute submission, to this mesmerizing leader.

Everyone seems a bit confused. This is the Governor, and yet he has such a gentle way about him. Some make the mistake of thinking, maybe he's not so tough after all!

Tinga decides to take advantage of this soft hearted person and make a few points for himself. "Excuse me, sir. Mister Sterben, we are just discussing what we need to do to rid ourselves of those Christians." Unfortunately, it doesn't get him anywhere.

Sterben continues on as if no one has spoken, and as far as he is concerned, no one has. Towering over the lectern, Sterben regains his composure and then speaks to the assembly. "Greetings, my fellow warriors, I am Governor Sterben. I have been sent here to help you warriors of the high priest, to put once and for all, an end to this Christian uprising. The lord is not pleased with what's been done so far. Obviously you're not taking your treacherous enemies serious enough." Wanting them to hang on his every word, he pauses to allow all he's said thus far to sink in really good and give them time to comprehend what he's trying to get across to them. His eyes radiating with a warmth, seeming to saturate their entire being as he gazes around the room. "There is a method to their madness. And you've yet to stop the source of their power. These **praying** people are the root of the problem. If they don't **pray**, then there will be **no power**. And thus we are in complete and absolute control. Now, does this clear things up for you? We have to stop the prayer **BEFORE** it starts." His manner has won him instant favoritism.

Warning. This Is A Test. This Is Only A Test.

They've been accustomed to everyone ordering them around like they have no brains. Now Governor Sterben is treating them more like equals, speaking to them with respect, and showing some consideration. Like dumb animals they are being used, they have no idea there is an ulterior motive to his craziness, also.

"Okay, my loyal and worthy fellow warriors, it's time for the Christians' final hour to begin. This is my plan." He sets them up to be slaughtered, hoping that maybe one or two of the Host of Heaven will be eliminated in the process, purely by accident of course.

The weather outside is a cold twenty degrees, but the trouble coming over the horizon is going to heat things up considerably. Sterben has the demonic clan stirred up to the boiling point. Egos inflated to enormous proportion, their hopes are high. The smell of Victory fills the lungs of each and every imp and demon. They've lied to themselves so often that this whopper of a tale seems to actually make sense. Go figure!!

Inside the operating room, Doctor Jeffreys and his surgical team have prepped their patient and are ready to begin the operation to stop the bleeding in Mitch's head.

Gloria Favors

Over on the dark side of town, Sterben has the masses hooting and howling like a bunch of wild animals. These destructive demons are wound up so tight, if they aren't let loose they could possibly destroy the hideout, and themselves, thus the mission would be a total loss. They're ready to do whatever it takes to be rid of these Christians. And that is exactly what the plan has been from the beginning. What would be the purpose of sending them one at a time? It is obvious to Sterben there isn't enough brains in the group to design a plan, follow orders, and have it go right. So he has the whole group going at once. Surely out of the two thousand, six hundred and forty three semi-intelligent demons of darkness, they can get rid of seventy or so Christians who know nothing about fighting. All they do is go to church. These are passive, gentle people. He is a mighty Governor of war. He's led massacres for centuries. He knows how to pull all the punches and deliver all the low blows. This will be a piece of cake for him. He is privy to the information that holds this battle plan together. He knows the heavenly host and the demons of darkness are a bit concerned about the big fuss over these few Christians, but orders have been given, time is short, and the ultimate plan is to rob the people of their power by robbing them of their prayer. This isn't about one person, one church, one town, or one state. This is a complete and all out war on the way of life as the christians at large now

Warning. This Is A Test. This Is Only A Test.

know it. Lucifer's plan to take over the world is as it has been from the beginning. Blinded by greed and self-glorification, he continues to work at achieving this unobtainable goal.

Above the hospital a cloud of prayer is rising through the roof like a huge glowing funnel cloud. It can be seen for miles. The Church family is on their knees. They've each been under attack with illness, financial problems, or any number of trials the enemy has thrown their way, but they know that the Word of God is true and tests are part of being a 'proven vessel of honor'. They aren't afraid of the battle; they know the Leader they follow has never before, nor will He ever, lose a battle or a war. This is war, and the army of God has called in its' reserves. When the devil and his devas mess with the Church, they better be ready for a serious battle.

Gunther is well aware that trouble is on its' way and he wants to be ready. "Warriors, I'm going to report what we've come up against and see what our Lord would have us do. Hold things together until I return. Strom I place you in charge of guarding Mitch, until I return."

"I am at your disposal comrade. Kreig can stand my post in my absence." He nods an affirmative nod to Kreig.

"We will see to it that all is guarded until your hasty return." Kreig says.

"I will return with orders from our Lord, and plans to end this battle." With that said, he is gone.

"**O**kay, my blood thirsty little demons, the time has come! You have proven yourselves ready to take on these Christians. Tinga, lead your army out to battle and spare no one. Today the victory will be on the side of darkness." Sterben has his job done, but, just for fun, he's tagging along to watch them destroy one another. This will leave him in control of the entire region, and he'll be free to appoint one of his soldiers to take over here. Greed and self-exaltation is the backbone of every imp and demon. A family trait, you could say, handed down to them from their father. Just as he himself couldn't and didn't resist challenging the throne of the MOST HIGH, his loyal subjects follow in his traitorous footsteps.

In heaven, Gunther receives his orders and is on his way back in a flash.

Warning. This Is A Test. This Is Only A Test.

As the horde of demons streak across the howling, snow covered sky, the plan is seemingly going fine. Jealousy isn't aware that first in the line is Bitterness. Standing next to Sterben is Envy, and Hatred will not put up with that when it finally comes to his attention. Heads will roll. Greed hasn't noticed that Tinga is having a private conversation with the unpopular demon, Death. When the spell of unity that Sterben has so skillfully spun wares off, and it will be any minute now, the imps will return to there normal, nasty selves, and this harmonious army will not last too much longer.

Bickering and crying can be heard within the first few miles of the journey. "I'm in the lead." Like a playground full of children, they begin to scratch and claw. "Who do you think you are?"

"Oh, no, you're not, I am." A war breaks out in their own camp.

Tinga is ready to kill them all himself and they aren't even halfway to their designated spot. Cursing and fighting, it is a mini war. They are defeating themselves before they ever meet their enemy. They've lost a good three hundred imps en route. As the hospital comes into view, everything comes to an abrupt, screeching halt. They can't believe their eyes. What is this huge glowing cloud that is coming out of the hospital's roof?

Sterben strokes their inflated egos with more lies. "Don't let this fool you, my warriors. It's only a trick. Look around, we have the numbers, the power, and the strength on our side. We will defeat these praying Christians this day." The mass of demons slowly resume their descent on the hospital.

Deuteronomy 32:39 See now that I, even I, am he, and there is no god with me: I kill, and I make alive; I wound, and I heal: neither is there any that can deliver out of my hand. (KJV)

1 Cor 15:54-55
54   So when this corruptible shall have put on incorruption, and this mortal shall have put on immortality, then shall be brought to pass the saying that is written, Death is swallowed up in victory.
55   O death, where is thy sting? O grave, where is thy victory?
(KJV)

Warning. This Is A Test. This Is Only A Test.

The Master Physician

10

In the hospital's dimly lit Chapel, a chilling wind announces, Death has entered the room. As a dark shrouded figure engulfs the room with its' hair raising presence, Kreig, Valek, Strom, and The Bishop, stand erect, unshaken and prepared. Until the official word is given, they are here to see to it that no boundaries are crossed. They know there's no need to panic, even Death must go through the Blood to obtain a life.

As the room empties of all its' little imps, the scratching, clawing, and fluttering of leathery wings, causes a tremendous distraction. They are making room for Death, with his extremely bad reputation preceding him, and his long cloak trailing behind him. He causes quite a stir.

Pastor McAllister rises to his feet. "We are not battling a condition, it's been revealed to me, we're battling hell itself. It is strengthening itself, and it's congregating within the walls of the hospital." He proclaims, with his hands raised toward Heaven.

"Death, you're about to be introduced to direct, and limitless power. If I were you I'd run and hide!" The Bishop cocks his head to one side and smiles. "Just a bit of advice."

Death snarls, "These powerless mortals do not intimidate me." Clutching the lapels of his cloak of arrogance, the demon glares at the prayer group kneeled on the floor. His black eyes, like deep, dark holes, illuminate the room with an eerie glow. As he exhales, a puff of choking, scarlet red smoke fills the room. "It is they who fear me."

"Okay, but don't say we didn't warn you." The Bishop snickers, shrugging his enormous shoulders.

The angelic warriors step aside, motion for him to step right up, and let the prayer warriors take charge of this demonic pest in their own way.

"Ladies, we need to bind together like never before. The scripture says we have power where any two or three agree on any one thing. I believe we are all agreeing that the enemy is here in full force, and that we have the power, at our disposal, to overcome through the name of **Jesus**. The best way I know to get the devil on the run is to quote God's Word and use His name to send him back where he came from." His voice is confident and his words are emphatic.

The demon covers his ears, flinches, and turns away when the Name of Jesus is spoken. His spider like arms fling his cascading cape tighter around his

Warning. This Is A Test. This Is Only A Test.

body, as though he would be shielded from the Word that is being spoken against him.

Victoria stands to her feet, lifts her hands to the Heavens, and proclaims, "Greater is **He** that is within us, than he that is in the world." She feels victory with every word that is spoken.

The demon hisses, and begins to groan. "You can not stop me!" He begins to tremble and quake.

Kreig can feel the power of the spoken Word invigorating his energy level. "We told you, but you wouldn't listen. They've only just begun!" The angelic host is enjoying this.

Mrs. McAllister adds to that, "Be sober, be vigilant; because your adversary the devil, as a roaring lion, walketh about, seeking whom he may devour. **I claim it to be so in Jesus name**."

Valek flexes his twenty-two inch biceps and proclaims, "we shall be victorious this night."

The demon Death can't stand the heat; he propels himself up, and out of sight. He's running with his tail tucked between his legs, back to the cowardly flock of demented imps.

"**He will** swallow up death in victory, and the **Lord GOD will** wipe away tears from off all faces." Pastor McAllister shouts.

"This night will go down in the pages of history as a mighty win for righteousness. These mortals would be astonished if they knew the influence their prayers were having on the spirit world." The Bishop declares, towering several feet above the rest of the warriors.

Cricket reports, "I am He that liveth, and was dead; and, behold, I am alive for evermore, Amen; and have the keys of hell and of death."

As Gunther makes his way through the snow filled sky, back to join his celestial brothers, he sees the glowing cloud over the hospital has doubled since he left only minutes ago. He's also aware of the newcomers; the glow of their beady eyes, and the stench of sin is hard to hide. He continues on as if nothing is wrong. He finds Kreig, Valek and The Bishop in the chapel, "My brothers, we have guests!" Gunther says in a matter of fact tone.

"Yes, the situation has changed considerably since you left." Valek replies, as he slowly looks around the room. "The prayer cover has also enlarged. Everything is in place, and we are sure to be victorious."

There are so many of the slimy little creatures, they are literally oozing out of the walls, and they aren't doing very well keeping quiet either.

"Our orders are to protect and deliver victory. So, whatever it takes, we are to keep the fiendish rebels from their task. The prayer support has grown as the enemy can well see by the enormous cloud ascending up to Heaven above the hospital. Yes Valek, you are right, we will not be defeated." Gunther directs the others, and at that they know what they are to do.

Warning. This Is A Test. This Is Only A Test.

"We should check on Strom?" Kreig suggests.

T inga, still a bit apprehensive about making the wrong move, is extremely cautious giving out the order to attack. He knows this is his big chance to show his skills in front of a Governor. He's faced these warriors on many occasions, and he's seen prayer clouds, but never before one so vast.
"What seems to be the trouble here, **Captain** Tinga?" Sterben so slyly encourages. He recognizes the selfishness Tinga displays, and knows to get what he wants, he must pretend to give Tinga what he longs for: Power.

That's all the coaxing that is needed. Tinga is ready for his promotion to Captain. "Go to your appointed duties and let's get this little scrimmage over with!" Tinga shouts with a new found authority.

I n the operating room the walls begin to gush forth little demons and imps, as more make their way into the hospital. Like swarming flies they fill every inch of the room.

Gunther, Kreig, Strom, Valek, and The Bishop, stand their ground. They feel assured of the outcome of this battle. They've witnessed the determination of the mortals, felt the effects the prayers are having on them personally, and have seen the enemy retreating as a direct result of the Name of Jesus being used.

"Okay, my friends, it's elimination time." Gunther commands.

They draw their shimmering swords from their sheaths, and with one swing, they are able to mow down the little critters as fast as they appear. It's like child's play. The enormous strength and stamina these warriors display is a direct result of the prayers being prayed.

Gunther appears to be playing a game instead of fighting a battle. In one hand he yields a sword, slashing and slicing, with the other, he swats demons like they are small flying insects.

Tinga has had enough of this game. He decides it's time for a real warrior to show these five angel boys, who possesses the strength. He calls together his best, most ruthless, fighting demons. "Get in there and put an end to this game!"

The opposition is getting a little tougher, but, it's nothing they can't handle. The weakest warrior the God of Heaven has to offer, is stronger and more efficient than the most powerful, forces of darkness could ever produce.

In the midst of all the battling, seemingly from out of nowhere, a brilliant light fills the operating room, and hovers over the operating table. The demonic legion is silent and paralyzed in their tracks. His angelic warriors bow in reverence. As the doctors work feverishly to save Mitch's life, the **King Of Kings And Lord Of Lords** steps into the room. With the hands of a skilled surgeon, as the room of

Warning. This Is A Test. This Is Only A Test.

silent warriors look on, the nail scarred hands reach into the middle of the procedure and put the final touch on the surgery. A specialist is needed, and, **'The Specialist'** is here. As silently as He appeared, He is gone. No talking, no explanation given. He has never been much on hanging around for the proverbial pat on the back. It is done, and He receives His gratification from the praises He hears coming from the lips of His children.

That is all the inspiration the angelic host needs to mop up this dirty little mess. The battle resumes in full force.

Tinga and his bunch can't retreat fast enough. Imps, demons, devas, devils, and every evil thing within the sound of their voice, retreats to the open sky.

Sterben is so disgusted by the pitiful display of warfare he's viewing, he leaves without a word.
Not to mention the fact that he knows he's been defeated and doesn't want to hang around chancing a confrontation with any of the Heavenly Host. After all, he knows the way things are going here, it won't be long before the imps completely wipe themselves out. No amount of encouragement he could offer will turn this malignant mission around.

Isaiah 14:12-15

12 How art thou fallen from heaven, O Lucifer, son of the morning! how art thou cut down to the ground, which didst weaken the nations!

13 For thou hast said in thine heart, I will ascend into heaven, I will exalt my throne above the stars of God: I will sit also upon the mount of the congregation, in the sides of the north:

14 I will ascend above the heights of the clouds; I will be like the most High.

15 Yet thou shalt be brought down to hell, to the sides of the pit. (KJV)

Warning. This Is A Test. This Is Only A Test.

The Retreat

11

Gunther and friends aren't going to let the enemy just walk out. This is the moment they've all been waiting for, the clean up crew is here. They've stood back and been more or less spectators in this entire ordeal. This is their chance to show the power and the might of the Great and Undefeated, King Of Glory. This is going to be a victory for Mitch, Victoria, the McAllisters, and Christians everywhere. With their bodies still bulging with the enormous energy the prayers of the saints has provided, their swords glistening, their focus set, and their purpose unified, they are set to charge the flock of retreating chickens, and make a quick work of the troublemakers.

From the Heavens above, the army of angelic warriors are encompassed about with a bright and brilliant light bursting through the cold, snow covered night sky. From the core of the funnel of light, comes a reassuring voice. "This night shall all the world know that my people which are called by my name, have humbled themselves, they have prayed, and I have healed their lands. Now, go forth and avenge my people of their adversaries."

Just the words they wanted to hear. In harmonious oneness, the Host shouts, **"To God Be The Glory and To The Lamb That Was Slain For The Sins Of The World."**

Gunther takes it upon himself to see to it that Sterben receives his just reward. He's heard many, most likely exaggerated, tales about this celebrated General of the dark forces. It is time he is personally introduced to the power of prayer, via Gunther's sword.

The Bishop wants to have the pleasure of saying, 'goodbye' to Tinga.

Kreig and Strom stand guard over the hospital. It's not likely that any of the fleeing troops will return, but stranger things have happened. When you're dealing with the devil, and his misguided sort, you are likely to see just about anything.

Across the stormy sky you can hear Valek's voice echo, in the true flavor of Texas, as he shouts, **"Remember The Cross And The Blood Of The Lamb,"** He's chasing a flock of the little underlings streaking across the sky.

The rewards of being patient are always so sweet.

Sterben is on his way out of town, retreating to his lair to hide, and he isn't looking back. He's not aware that Gunther is overtaking him and has no intention of going back until the job is done. Total,

Warning. This Is A Test. This Is Only A Test.

and complete, annihilation of all opposing factions is the goal of this Heaven sent warrior. Continuing to feel the power of prayer supplying every fiber of his being, with raw energy, he charges on.

From their vantage point on top of the hospital, Kreig and Strom watch the contest, and provide the cheering section for their friend, Gunther.

With his majestic sword drawn, Gunther calls out to Sterben, "The fun's just beginning. You can't leave the party yet." His broad smile reveals his playful, but mischievous side.

Sterben turns to face his pursuing opponent. Pulling his sword, that bears the blood of the innocent, from it's sheath, he eagerly accepts the challenge. "I had no idea you considered yourself a match for my skill and cunning. I count it an honor to own the sword that will put an end to your pathetic existence."

Kreig and Strom send out a cheer, "Go, Gunther."

The prayer groups continue to pray and supply strength to the Heavenly Host.

With glares that could kill, the two unevenly matched rivals lunge at one another, like bullets being shot out of a forty-four magnum. Sterben is hurled backwards with a sharp jab from Gunther's explosive right cross. That proves to only make him madder. Gunther just smiles and challenges him to try again.

Sterben bounces back and takes a swipe at Gunther with his ill-match sword.

Gunther delivers a well placed jab with his trusty sword, into Sterben's side. Sterben roars like a wounded lion, grabbing his oozing side.

"I truly expected a little more competition from the Governor of Military Forces. Perhaps I've caught you on a bad day." Gunther is being slightly antagonistic.

As the two are sizing one another up they continue to shuffle around the sky in a circle, watching, waiting, for that moment when the other is off guard.

Gunther's wanting to savor the moment, taking him apart one piece at a time.

Sterben is trying desperately to save his worthless hide, and get out of there as quickly as possible.

Wincing with pain from his pierced side, he growls. "It is you who must surely be having a bad day. It is not one of mine at deaths' door in that hospital. Was it not your personal responsibility to keep him from harms way?" His words are meant to cut as deeply as he has been cut.

"It was, and will continue to be, my honor to guard Mitch Arrington with my life if need be. For your information, he is not at deaths' door. Our superior cunning and abilities defeated your inferior flock of cowardice demons. By the power and authority of our Lord Jesus Christ, we have this day been made victors."

"You tell him Gunther!" Kreig shouts.

The two continue to circle and glare at one another.

Warning. This Is A Test. This Is Only A Test.

"You boast and give yourself way too much credit, my winged warrior, but how are you at demonstrating these skills that you so easily talk about?" He's trying to bluff his way out of this predicament, but only manages to talk himself into another round. He lunges at Gunther, but misses.

"It is not of myself that I speak boastfully, but of the Sovereign Savior, Jesus Christ. The name itself has sent your best running into the night like scalded dogs." His chest inflates with pride to be called to battle for such a cause.

"Spoken like a true winner!" Strom yells. "Finish him Gunther."

"Enough of this child's play. I'm ready to finish what you have started." With the roar of an angry beast, Sterben's nostrils flare like that of a charging bull, his massive body shakes with the force building up inside of him, and he screams out. **"This day you shall know the power of darkness."** The shaking can be felt on the ground below as Sterben takes off. It sounds like the engines of a stealth bomber. He continues to scream and declare victory over the Christians. **"Your day is coming, I will never give up!"**

Kreig and Strom feel the mounting force as it builds, shaking the roof of the hospital beneath them. They struggle to stand to their feet, not wanting to miss any of this.

Gunther knows all power is given unto God in heaven and on earth, and the enemy only has brute force. There is nothing for him to be concerned about. With the patience of Job, he waits. Just as they are within a few feet of one another, Gunther runs his sword through the middle of Sterben. And then it is Gunther's turn to shout. **"Another victory for the Most High has been obtained this night**." His cry of victory is heard for hundreds of miles.

Kreig and Strom shout and rejoice with Gunther. "Truth and justice have prevailed."

On the outskirts of town, Tinga is trying his best to outrun The Bishop. He wants no part of this huge fellow. But The Bishop is too smart, too fast, and too tricky, to play chase with this snake. Ducking out of sight and slipping around the side of Tinga, The Bishop comes out in front of the scared rabbit. Popping up in front of him, Tinga runs directly into the massive warrior.

Stumbling for words, as he desperately tries to throw it into reverse, "Now, now, you don't want me I'm---." He continues to scramble backwards.

The Bishop stays in Tinga's face, taunting him. "I - don't - want - you....what? I don't want you tormenting anymore, is that what you were about to say? Or maybe I don't want you in my face any more!" He is giving him the scare of his life.

"I'm going, I'm going!" Tinga tries to back stroke out of The Bishops' reach.

"Yes, you're going somewhere all right, but not by your own power. I'm sending you on an all expense paid, one way trip, non-stop flight. How does

Warning. This Is A Test. This Is Only A Test.

that sound?" The Bishop continues to stay right in Tinga's ugly face as he backs away.

"Now look, I'm not in charge here. This wasn't my idea. You want Sterben, he's a much bigger catch." Tinga never has been much of a brave heart. "I'll just go and let you get about your business." He turns to flee.

"Oh, no, you don't, my little troublemaker, not so fast, we still have one more thing to do." The Bishop grabs him by his scrawny neck, and shouts, **"To God Be The Glory"** and gives it a twisting squeeze. That is the end of that.

V alek is having a grand time. The little imps are flying across the sky like shooting stars, trying to stay out of his reach. They are just foolish enough to try his hand, but not competent enough to do any significant damage to this mighty warrior. He chases a while, then he grabs a few and throws them out across the vast galaxy. Gunther and The Bishop, finished with their duties, come to see if he needs any help. Help is not needed, but he did offer to let them join in the fun. He isn't ready to leave just yet.

Hebrews 11:34-35

34 Quenched the violence of fire, escaped the edge of the sword, out of weakness were made strong, waxed valiant in fight, turned to flight the armies of the aliens.

35 Women received their dead raised to life again:

(KJV)

Warning. This Is A Test. This Is Only A Test.

Victory

12

Victoria, the McAllisters, and Cricket, hear the door to the little Chapel open; they can see a silhouette standing in the door way. Squinting their eyes, they try to focus on the persons' face, but it's hard to see with the florescent lights from the hallway shining directly in their eyes, after being in the dimly lit chapel for so long.

"It's Esther." A soft voice whispers. "Mitch is in the recovery room. Would you like to go in and see him now?"

Victoria doesn't take the time to reply, she just gets up and follows Esther. As she enters the recovery room, she knows something wonderful has happened. Mitch has such a healthy countenance that you wouldn't know he'd just come through a serious surgery. As she gently takes his hand, tears once again fill her eyes. "Thank God, you're all right." Tears of joy stream down her weary face.

Mitch opens his eyes slightly and smiles at her like he'd just gotten up from a well deserved nap. "Honey, Jesus was here!" He whispers, his voice is a little raspy.

If only they could really know about the mighty battle they've just won. But they have no idea of the boundless number of demons that have been defeated, about how close they all came to being a page in history if they'd let down their guard for only a second. There is no way they'll ever know that they had a personal visit by the greatest Physician ever known. In time, it will be made known the mighty victories they've won.

For a short time, the seat occupied by Tinga, the prince of this town, will be vacant, and the control that was once held by the spirit of darkness will have to be regained by another. Until that time comes, like true soldiers of the cross, the saints can rejoice over the knowledge they provided, the prayer cover when it was needed, and victory has been won. The Church of the Living God will not be defeated. The war will again be fought another day, in another town.

Outside, the snow is still falling, the wind is still blowing like a gale, but inside, everything has returned to calm. The power of prayer has prevailed over darkness.

Doctor Jeffreys clears his throat as he comes in to tell Mrs. Arrington how well the surgery has gone. "Mrs. Arrington, I don't quite know how to tell you, but your husband has been given a miracle this night. His condition going into surgery was extremely critical. I wasn't very hopeful that he'd pull through. During surgery his vital signs bottomed out, and at first it appeared we were not going to be able to revive him. But just as we were about to give up, everything changed. His vital signs returned to normal, his coloring was perfect, and the bleeding stopped like it had been turned off by a faucet. I've never experienced that before in my life. The surgery went great. It went smoother than I ever remember it going before. If I didn't know better I'd say I had an extra set of hands. I'm grateful for whatever happened to turn things around. I don't like losing patients. As you can see, he's going to be just fine. The ribs will be a little problem for a while, until he gets accustomed to the bandages. Anyway, I just wanted to let you know how things went, so you can rest a little better tonight."

The couple just smiles as Doctor Jeffreys clamors over the miracle they've been given. "Thank you, Doctor Jeffreys." Victoria says. "I appreciate all you've done. You are right about one thing, we have most definitely received a miracle tonight." She clings to Mitch's hand. "Doctor Jeffreys, do you believe in the power of prayer?" Victoria can't let this miracle fade away; she wants the world to know what God has done for her and her husband.

"I thought I did, but after tonight I feel certain there's more to this than I am aware of." Doctor Jeffreys is still in a state of amazement. "I'd really like to hear more about this miracle when you're feeling better and have rested some."

"Doctor, would you show Reverend McAllister and his wife in? I know they want to see him before they have to go." Victoria asks.

"I'll see to it that they are shown in. I'll see you first thing in the morning." He pats Mitch's foot and walks out into the hallway a happier man.

"Oh Mitch, God has done such mighty, and amazing things for us. I'm so happy that you are going to be okay." She can't stop crying. "I can't wait to tell you all that's happened!"

Still groggy from the surgery, Mitch just smiles and closes his eyes.

Reverend and Mrs. McAllister make their way into the room and around to the side of the bed, across from Victoria. "Victoria, how is he feeling?"

"Well just see for yourself, he looks wonderful. The doctor says he's doing unbelievably well, and God's already using this as a tool for winning souls to Him." Victoria is beaming with joy.

"God is most definitely a miracle worker. It is getting late and the roads aren't going to get any better, so we are going to ease out and go home." Reverend McAllister smiles and grips Mitch's hand. "We'll be praying for you."

"I appreciate you coming more than I can say." Victoria reaches for Mrs. McAllister and gives her a big hug.

"We'll see you tomorrow, Lord willing." Mrs. McAllister says, as they make their way out.

The McAllisters feel sure that everything is under control. The battling is over, for now. It is one more win for the Christians. The Church Triumphant. They stop back by the emergency room waiting area to say goodnight to Cricket, and then make their way home.

Warning. This Is A Test. This Is Only A Test.

"I'm sure it'll be okay for you to go in now and see Mitch." Reverend McAllister encourages.

"I will, and thank you for coming." Cricket waves goodbye and races down the hall to the recovery room. She wants to see the results of their prayers, and view first hand the miracle God has done.

Victoria and Cricket sit talking for about half an hour, rejoicing over the blessings they have received. Noticing the hour, Cricket decides she better try to make her way home before she has to get up, and go to work. She says goodnight, and she's on her way out into the cold, dark, snowy night, with a heart full of joy and a song on her lips.

Victoria spends the night at the hospital. As she finally gives in and closes her eyes, she fells that someone is looking at her. Opening her eyes, she sees a radiant glow in the middle of the room. It moves toward her and smiles. She knows then, that they have been visited by an angel of God. She rests better than she's rested in days.

Early the next morning, she calls her mother to let her in on the grand and glorious night they've had.

"Hello." Mr. Miller says, wiping jelly from his mouth.

"Hey, Dad, how is the great hunter this morning?" The smile on her face is conveyed through her happy voice.

"I'm fine. The question is, how are you and Mitch?"

Ruby overhears the conversation, "How is he? Is that Victoria?" Ruby clamors.

Knowing he'll never be able to hear Victoria over Ruby's barrage of questions, he lets Ruby find out what's going on. "Here's your mother Victoria, she wants to talk to you." He hands Ruby the phone, and gets back to eating his breakfast.

"Victoria, how is everything?" Ruby's wiping her hands on her sunflower print apron.

"Oh, Mom, everything is just wonderful! I have so much to tell you about." Her voice tells it all.

"Did the surgery go okay?"

"Oh Mom that's the best part of all! We've had a miraculous miracle take place! Mitch's surgery went great. The doctor even commented to us personally how amazed he was. Hold on a minute Mom, there's someone at the door."

While she's still on the line, she is greeted with news that Mitch is being moved to his own room.

"Thank you!" She's excited even more. "Mom, I'm gonna let you go. Mitch is being moved to his own room. I'll call you back shortly."

"Okay Hun, and thank you for calling us with the good news. We are so proud for you both."

"Oh, Mom, tell the kids I said hello, and I'll see them soon."

"I will, now you go 'tend to Mitch."

Gathering her things, she hurries to the elevator and happens to meet Mitch as he is being rolled out of I. C. U. on his way to his room. "Hey guy! How's it going?"

Mitch smiles and reaches out to hold her hand. "Couldn't be better if I tried."

"You had a pretty exciting night last night!"

Warning. This Is A Test. This Is Only A Test.

In room 27, the nurses roll Mitch's bed to the middle of the room, hook up his monitors and I. V. bags. "Doctor Jeffreys will be in early this morning," one of the nurses remarks.

"Thank you." Victoria says as she stands in the doorway waiting to tell Mitch all the wonderful things that have transpired.

The nurses put the final touches, getting him settled into his room, and leave the couple alone.

"Come here, lady. I need a hug." He reaches out to Victoria.

She races to his side. "Oh Mitch, I have so much to tell you." She begins to cry tears of relief. The battle's over, overjoyed that she has her husband to hold, and happy that she knows everything has worked for their good.

Mitch gently raises his masculine hands up, places them on her dainty shoulders, and pushes her up so that he can see her face. With a serious look on his face he tries to relay to her everything he's felt. "Victoria, you won't believe what I dreamed. It must have been during surgery." He wipes the tears from her soft cheeks. "I was standing in the middle of a battle field, and there seemed to be a war of some kind going on all about me. Bombs exploding, yelling, fighting, and shouting was coming from every direction. Then, like the first light of day, the field was illuminated, and standing directly over the top of me was a huge, radiant angel. He smiled at me and said, "I'll Never Leave You Nor Forsake You." I knew then everything was gonna be okay. It seemed so real."

As she sat on the side of his bed listening to his story, a tear comes to her eye. "Honey, it wasn't a dream. We've been battling this war for a long time. The final round started two nights ago when you couldn't sleep. The battle is over, and we've won. We've staked our claim on this town in the name of Jesus, and He came to our defense when we were under the big guns. The enemy tried to destroy our faith and confidence, but the tables have been turned."

Mitch recovers remarkably well. His stay in the hospital is a good opportunity to tell everyone how good God has been to him. He now has a Texas size miracle to tell about.

The guys from the shop are all really touched by his miracle. The last time they'd seen him he was in really bad shape. They'd not expected to see him alive, and they never dreamed he'd be doing this good.

The phones are ringing around the world. The call goes out about the miracle God has performed on Mitch Arrington. Another faith booster. It isn't time to quit praying. It is time to proclaim all out war on the devil and his imps.

G unther is standing a lot taller these days. He has always been impressed by the courage and stamina of these mortals who fight so valiantly for what they believe in. The Arringtons, and their

Warning. This Is A Test. This Is Only A Test.

fellow believers of Shepherd County, have been through a lot in the past few days, not to mention the past months. He knows these people will go on to do a great and mighty work. He looked into the face of courage when Daniel was in the lions' den; David, when he faced Goliath; and today, he saw it in the lives of these Christians. They've all been tested and tried. One more time, he is proud to say he's fought alongside true winners. The days ahead are going to be a greater challenge to these Christian people, but the battle is to those who endure. Gunther and his friends will be there as long as there is a battle to be fought, and prayer to supply the power.

Onward Christian soldiers.

I John 5:4-5

4   For whatsoever is born of God overcometh the world: and this is the victory that overcometh the world, even our faith.

5   Who is he that overcometh the world, but he that believeth that Jesus is the Son of God?

(KJV)